How ~~NOT~~ to Date a DRAGON

CAUTIONARY TAILS BOOK TWO

LANA KOLE

CONTENTS

CONTENT INFORMATION

For a complete list of content information pertaining to How
Not to Date a Dragon, please refer to my website.

For those of us still searching.

1. NEW IN TOWN

"I'm not late!"

The crowd inside the local bar froze, merriment pausing as they turned toward him when the door slammed shut, encasing him in the dimly lit interior. Balancing the cake plate in hand, Milo stepped forward, only to come to a stop as the silence stretched on.

His saving grace was a familiar, age lined face with white peppered jowls, grin in place as the human stepped forward to take the cake from him, peering through the plastic cover. "Oh, it's beautiful!"

The party resumed, volume cranking up to eleven as the bar cheered. John patted him on the shoulder and ushered him forward, and as they made their way to the bar, Milo received several congratulatory claps on the back.

"It's just a cake," he muttered as a barmaid—*no, that's not what they're called these days*—bartender passed him an amber filled glass.

"But it's my *wife's* birthday cake, man! And you weren't late this time, so I think that deserves a beer. Drink up," John told him, smile wide and bright and eyes a little twinkly. "She'll be here in about ten minutes, so there's even time to spare! I couldn't be more proud of you."

"Listen, John, the mix was from a box—"

"Hush, none of that. You made it, put it together, and wrote her name on it in that fancy writing. Stop selling yourself short and drink your beer."

"Yeah, don't be a dick," the bartender agreed with a wink.

Milo acquiesced with only a slight grumble, and sipped his beer. The local brew was his weakness and they all knew it. Fuckers.

"I'm gonna go set this on the pedestal it deserves—"

"We're just gonna *eat* it—"

"—and wait for Patty. She's gonna love it, Milo, I'm telling you."

He sighed, setting his glass down with a quiet clink. "You're gonna make me blush if you keep saying shit like that."

But John had already stepped away, setting the cake in the center of the bar, surrounded by festive cups and matching tiny plates and napkins. A strand of lights was strung along the ceiling, casting the tidy bartop in a soft glow. Laughter echoed around the room, growing louder by the minute as they anticipated Patty's arrival.

It was no small thing, celebrating the two bar owners, hence the crowd. Every table was filled and all hands were on deck to make sure the drinks kept flowing.

These parties only happened twice a year, and in a town this small, it was a big deal. One not to be missed.

Milo stepped away from the bar to make room for the next eager patron and nodded politely at the man, a regular at the bakery. Milo didn't know his real name, so he was forever referred to as Cupcake Guy.

Came in every Friday for a dozen for his office. Milo couldn't remember where he worked or what the man did in his office, but he remembers stuffing a white box full of his finest. At least until he'd finally hired someone to help with the counter. Now he didn't have to concern himself with peopling.

Milo loved these little get-togethers as much as the next, but he preferred standing over a hot ass stove, ovens going full blast, to making small talk with every fucker that walked in for a sweet treat.

"Oh my *heavens!*"

Speaking of sweet…

Milo turned, grin curling his lips as Patty leaned over the bar to eye the cake he'd made. He'd lied. It wasn't a box cake. He'd made that shit in the bakery, had been planning the design and the lettering for nearly two weeks.

Patty's eyes glimmered with tears in the low lighting as she lifted her gaze to eye the full bar, now filled with shouts of excitement and big, uncoordinated shouts of *happy birthday, Patty!*

She laid a hand over her heart, the other brushing over her cheek. As if this year was any more a surprise than the year before that, and the year before that, and so on.

And like every year, she turned, arms outstretched to yank her husband into a bear hug until John's face turned a little red from the lack of air. She released him with a loud clap of laughter, framed his red cheeks with her palms, and gave him a smooch. The whole bar whistled, and Milo's grin widened.

How fucking sweet were they?

Having been around the bend a few hundred years, Milo knew how hard it was to find your person, and Patty and John?

Yeah, they'd been lucky, the love between them clear as day and in abundance to last a lifetime.

Crazy how some humans could find it in a third of the time he'd been alive. *When would it be* my *fucking turn?*

Patty turned to the exuberant crowd with a smile. "Where the fuck is Milo, eh?"

Trying to duck into the corner hadn't worked, and he was pulled back up to the bar by the smiling faces of the crowd. His shoulders would be sore after tonight, what with all the back pats and hair ruffles.

"Okay, okay!" he shouted, and sidled up to the bar. "Happy birthday Patty," he said once he was within ear shot.

"Did you make this?"

As if he hadn't made her cake the last five years in a row.

"Someone had to."

"Is it my favorite?"

"Coconut cream with pineapple curd, of course it's your favorite."

Coconut was a bitchy flavor to work with, but he'd perfected it *just* for Patty.

Damned humans. How dare they be so endearing.

John? He was easier.

Dark, rich chocolate with richer ganache.

Patty leaned across the bar and pulled Milo into a hug, but at their angle he ended up with his head crushed into her bosom. Milo patted her on the shoulder, everyone around them chuckling.

It was such a warm place. The bar, the town, the people. *Not* Patty's bosom.

"There's a new face over by seat six," Patty murmured by his ear. "Maybe you should check that out for us."

A new face? Around here?

Milo's interest was piqued, and he nodded before Patty released him with a warning. "No bloodshed on my birthday unless absolutely necessary. Got it?"

He nodded once more, and Patty gave him a pat on the cheek before she cheered with the nearby patrons.

Rarely were there new faces in town. Not as remote and

removed as they were from the rest of the world. Off the beaten path, some might say.

Nah. You didn't just stumble upon their valley.

As the resident dragon, he'd been keeping this town safe for quite a few lifetimes. He wasn't gonna stop now.

The bartender poured him another beer, and he gratefully accepted it, not bothering to protest again. He knew better.

Milo backed away from the bar, letting other friends crowd the birthday girl as he beelined for his empty table in the back. It was near the exit, and he could keep an eye on the patrons.

And the newcomer.

He stood out like a sore thumb.

How did I miss him upon arrival?

Even from here, across the dimly lit bar, he could see the far-too-many layers he was wearing for such a balmy evening. Milo couldn't say he didn't look absolutely intriguing in them, especially with that beanie, but really? A bit overkill, wasn't it?

From his ever-reserved table, Milo could catch glances of him from an angle. The strong jaw, the wisps of hair that peeked from beneath the beanie. He was wearing a black coat that stopped at his knees, revealing the brown combat boots, of which he had one kicked up on a rung of his bar stool. The rest of him was hidden by the oversized coat.

Milo sipped his beer, waiting... waiting...

The stranger lifted his head, eyes scanning the bar. The too casual expression he regarded the crowd with wouldn't have seemed so suspicious if his simple *presence* wasn't suspicious enough. He went back to nursing the drink on the bar in front of him, giving it a slow spin as he stared down at the amber ale.

Maybe he was just passing through. Maybe his vehicle broke down and he simply had to wait out the evening while it was repaired. Milo could give him the benefit of the doubt.

Either way, it couldn't hurt to… *talk* to him, could it?

Milo tilted his glass back again, realizing he'd made it to the end of his second beer with all his internal musing. With a sigh, he eyed the bar, wondering if he was brave enough to make it back through all the intoxicated humans for another drink.

The bartender who'd served him the first two times caught his eye over the heads of the patrons, winked, and made their way to the stranger.

Milo's eyes widened, and he was already shaking his head by the time the bartender sat a familiar looking ale down in front of the stranger. Watched in slight horror as he lifted his head, listened, and glanced over his shoulder.

Milo couldn't melt into the chair fast enough, and was ensnared in his gaze, the tilt of his lips. He nodded, wrapped a slim hand—oh my god, were those fingerless gloves?—around the glass, and pushed away from the bar.

He was helpless to do little more than watch as he weaved through the crowd, drinks held high to avoid any wild elbows. By the time the glasses clinked down on the table, Milo had composed himself from the mortification. Barely.

"I was told to deliver this to you," he said in greeting, pushing the amber filled glass toward him. Yes. Those *were* fingerless gloves.

"Thanks," Milo said, raising his voice to be heard over the noise level. Oh this wasn't *fair*.

The stranger was hot. Like, *so* hot. His button up shirt was opened deep, revealing a long pale strip of his sternum, and framing it all was a harness that Milo could have sworn had the shine of leather to it. Milo tried to appear casual, and not like he was about to swallow his own tongue. "First time here and they're already putting you to work, huh?"

He nodded, helping himself to the other seat at his high table. "Seems that way. Different type of hospitality than I'm used to."

"Oh yeah? Where's that?" Milo asked.

Smooth.

He arched a brow at him, sipping his own drink. "Around."

Milo's suspicions were not subsiding, despite the beguiling curiosity in the stranger's gaze. A gaze framed by the thickest feathering of eyelashes.

Milo guessed he could forgive whoever failed to mention the *hot* part of dark and mysterious.

It was at this moment that Milo realized he'd been sitting in silence, proverbially checking out the stranger for the past several minutes.

Fucking embarrassing.

"It's a lively crowd tonight," he said, if only to say *something*.

"I can tell. Patty's birthday, right?" the stranger asked before sipping the beer.

With a nod, Milo tried not to stare so hard. "Her and her husband own the bar. It's kind of a big deal around here."

"You made the cake, I take it?"

Milo hummed. "Caught that, did you?"

His smirk was nothing less than devastating. "Hard not to."

After another sip of beer, Milo announced, "I run the local bakery. Keep everyone stocked up on sweets. It's kind of my thing."

The stranger cocked his head, as if this information puzzled him. "You... bake?"

Milo's lips twitched. "Yeah. That's what you do when you run a bakery."

"So let me get this straight," he began, taking a sip of his beverage before returning the glass to the table with a clink and leaned closer, until Milo caught his scent, all lemongrass and leather and salt. "You look like *that*." He gestured to him with a wave of his hand. "Run a bakery, *and* bake cakes for cute old ladies on their birthday."

Milo's lips twitched. "Don't let Patty hear you say that. You'll be banished."

"Do you wanna take this… elsewhere?" he asked, and Milo arched a brow as the volume in the bar rose to unbearable.

"And miss this beautiful choir?"

The off-key happy birthday song filled the bar, bounced from wall to wall and back again, echoing louder in the enclosed space. Jovial laughter filled in the quiet moments, and Milo parted his lips, singing out the final happy birthday to Patty.

As the bar erupted into cheers, he grabbed the stranger's hand and abandoned his beer on the bartop, pulling him along.

Thankfully the exit was right near his table, and the warm summer night welcomed him with open arms as the back door closed with an offensive metal slam.

A few seconds too late, Milo heard the jangle of metal and felt the cold clasp of something heavy around his wrist.

No…

He turned back to the stranger with some sort of choked noise in his throat. "Excuse me?"

Snapping his gaze to his wrist, he took in the old, tarnished metal and the fancy symbols engraved. His eye twitched as he followed the chain to the wrist belonging to his captor.

"Is this some new age kink I haven't learned about yet?" he tried.

The stranger sputtered, taking a step back before the

chain pulled at them both. Clearing his throat, the stranger stepped forward again so his wrists lay limp at their sides.

He was close enough Milo could make out the hazel specks in his eyes, barely lit by the lamplight from the parking lot. In the next second, he pulled a knife from his pocket, and held it to Milo's throat. The sharp edge barely bit into his skin, and he didn't move.

"You didn't even flinch," he said, sounding disappointed.

Milo scoffed. "Well it's kind of counterproductive to cuff us together and then stab me. What, like you're gonna drag my limp body around?"

But that didn't mean he liked being threatened. He wasn't into *that* kink thank you very much.

In a swift move, Milo brought his forearm up—the one uncuffed—and knocked the blade away, hearing the clink as it bounced against the asphalt. The stranger—Milo should really learn his name at some point—gasped before blocking his punch with his forearm in an impressively agile movement.

Milo's wrist barely brushed the top of his head as he ducked as well, and the beanie fell off, landing unceremoniously on the ground. A swath of chopped, dark hair fell, spreading around his features. It seemed like everything was in slow motion, and were those… sparkles surrounding the stranger? Or just dust reflecting the light from the buzzing light post?

In Milo's moment of besotted distraction, the stranger swiped another knife at him and Milo jumped back as far as the cuff would let him.

"Come on, man!" Milo griped.

The stranger paused, barely noticeable if Milo hadn't been staring so intently. "Wrong. I'm nonbinary, fuckface."

Milo's lips parted in surprise, then morphed into contrition.

"Oh shit, I'm sorry, uh..." he paused, dipping his head in their direction, waiting for a name.

"Xander," they said automatically, eyes widening as they stared at him. "You're... apologizing."

Milo cocked his head to the side. "Well, yes. That's usually what you do when you misgender someone, isn't it?"

Xander lifted their joined hands, rattling the chain between them. "I just handcuffed you!"

And somehow that fact didn't make them any less attractive.

What the fuck was wrong with him?

To make it worse, Xander lifted their hand and ran it through their hair, gathering it back from their face briefly before it fell again in haphazard pieces around their sharp cheekbones.

"Yes, thank you for informing me," Milo answered, lips twitching at their exasperation. "Uhm, if I may..."

Xander's expression said he may *not*, but listen, Milo had made it this far, okay?

"Why, exactly, did you cuff us together?"

He was lucky to dodge the *second* knife Xander pulled from probably one of those thousand damned pockets on that stupidly warm jacket.

As he pulled away with a yelp, it tugged Xander's balance off, and they stumbled after him. Milo, like the gentleman he was, caught them before they could hit the ground. One palm was cupped at the back of their neck, while the cuffed hand slid around their waist.

"Get off me, asshole!" they hissed, eyes flaming with annoyance, and Milo frowned before—

"Fine." And promptly let them drop to the ground.

2. TANGLED UP

Xander glared up at the dragon, the sting in their palm a dull throb from where they'd tried to catch themself on the asphalt. *Any*thing was better than the dragon's stupid arms wrapped around them.

The dragon leaned down, nostrils flaring as he met their gaze. "Okay fine, you wanna play it like that? What's stopping me from killing you, searching your pockets, finding the key, and getting myself out of these?" he asked, voice low and dangerous as he jangled their joined hands.

"I'd like to see you try," Xander forced out through gritted teeth.

Fucking dragons.

They tensed, ready to react appropriately and survive this encounter no matter what. But the dragon, Milo, didn't move. Only continued to stare down at them. Was he sizing them up for a snack? Calculating how long it would take to gnaw their arm off to get the cuff free?

Milo did none of those things. He huffed, a breath of air escaping his nostrils before he sighed, and held his uncuffed hand out to them, palm up.

Xander darted their gaze from the hand to his put-upon expression, and back again.

"Just take it, for crying out loud," he muttered.

With a glare, Xander knocked his hand aside and stood, keeping as much space between them as was comfortable.

"Now what?" Milo asked.

Xander suddenly missed the old days, when killing dragons wasn't so forbidden. *So* much easier than this need for… diplomacy. "Take me to your treasure hoard and we'll call it a day. No bloodshed necessary."

"And if I don't?" he challenged, a glint in his eye that Xander couldn't quite decipher.

Xander rattled the single foot of chain between them. "Recognize the runes on these bad boys? You're not going anywhere until I get what I want, *dragon*."

Fine, maybe diplomacy wasn't Xander's best virtue.

Milo's gaze suddenly dipped, scanning over their body before flicking back to their gaze. "All that seems more of a problem for you than it does me, *hunter*."

Heat flooded Xander's chest, and they took a deep, slow breath to curb the anger rising hot beneath the surface. "It *will* bother you the longer it takes us to get these cuffs off. You're telling me your skin isn't already itching just from the *idea* of your dragon being locked away?"

The dragon's expression hardened. *Got him.*

Before Xander could even celebrate—silently—Milo ran a hand through his shoulder-length hair and smoothed out whatever annoyance may have shown through.

"Name's Milo, by the way, not Dragon. So, like, are we getting a rideshare or something?" he asked.

"Why would we need a rideshare?" Xander hissed. Trying, not very successfully, to curb their temper.

"Why not? You expect me to drive a motorcycle with us cuffed like this? Not fucking likely," Milo scoffed.

Xander cocked their head, gut tightening with something close to… embarrassment. "You drive a motorcycle?"

They *knew* Milo had a car. Why the fuck wasn't he driving it?

"Yes. Of course. Have you seen the backroads here? They're fucking gorgeous."

This man… was talking about the scenic routes while Xander had him handcuffed. And intended to steal his treasure hoard.

They frowned. "Are you not taking me seriously, dude? What's your problem?"

The dragon blinked back at them. "What's *my* problem? You're the one who's got a problem! You handcuffed me!"

"Yes, that's my point!" They waved their cuffed arm in the air, tugging his along with it. "Why aren't you pissed? Trying to gnaw my arm off or something?"

His nose wrinkled. Wrinkled! In a way that made the laugh lines around his eyes crinkle. "Well, that just sounds unappetizing."

"You're a fuckin— Ugh!" They ran their unoccupied hand through their hair, cursing and leaning down to snatch their beanie off the ground before stuffing it into their back pocket.

"So… are we getting a rideshare, or what?"

"Yes! Yes we're getting a fucking rideshare, Jesus!"

"Hmm, close. My name is Milo, remember?"

Xander sucked in a deep breath, begging whatever god there was for a bit of patience. Just a smidge.

"I take it you don't have a car either?"

Face reddening with far more than anger, Xander murmured, "No, I drive a fucking bike as well."

Milo snorted. Composed himself. Tilted his head in a way that reminded them of a puppy dog. "Sorry. What was that?"

"I drive a bike too! Fuck."

"Ah. Didn't think this through that well, did you?"

Xander snarled and stepped forward, backing Milo into the wall of the bar and snapped, "Shut *up*!"

Milo nodded, eyes wide. "Yep. Shutting up."

None of this was going to plan. Absolutely none of it. Tugging their phone out of their pocket, Xander pulled up the rideshare app and swallowed their pride. It went down like a glass of nails, but they ordered a car and huffed.

"I can't fucking believe this," they hissed.

"As far as I can tell, you're not the one who just got surprise handcuffed. What do you have to be surprised about?"

Xander lifted their head to glare at him. "What happened to shutting up?"

He shrugged. "I'm incapable. It's a disease."

Xander considered killing him. If only for a split second. Unfortunately, they needed him alive if only so he could point them in the direction of his dragon's hoard. So breathe —and incessantly talk—he must, at least for a few more hours.

"What's the plan here?" Milo asked.

"*Why* would I tell you that?" Xander seethed, knocking their head back into the brick of the building.

"What else are we gonna do to pass the time while we wait for the car?"

"Sit in silence. Contemplate what we did to get us to this unfortunate point in our lives."

The dragon hummed. "Might be unfortunate for you. From where I'm standing, it's not looking quite so bad."

Xander cracked one eye open and found Milo's gaze locked on them, an appreciative gleam in his eye.

"Do you want me to carve your eyes out of your skull? You don't need them for that much longer."

Milo's dark eyes widened before he averted them to the ground. If his lips twitched—which wouldn't be very smart of him, considering—he covered it with his fist. If the cough was disguising a chuckle, Xander would rather not know.

He wouldn't be laughing much longer, anyhow.

Fucking dragons.

The silence stretched on, and Xander enjoyed the bliss.

But like most good things, it didn't last.

"So you're after the hoard, yeah? What if I don't have one?" Milo questioned.

Xander caressed the hilt of the dagger in their belt, hidden by their jacket.

"Wouldn't be the first hunter they sent after me."

Their fingers paused at the tip of the handle, the only reaction they allowed themself.

"I didn't kill them or anything," Milo rushed to add, jangling their connected wrists as he waved his hands frantically. "Just… My hoard doesn't have anything of use to you guys."

When Xander didn't give him a reaction, he continued. "I mean, unless I'm incorrect. It *was* the Hunters of Obscure Artifacts who sent you, yes?"

Xander wasn't alarmed like Milo clearly wanted them to be. The HOA wasn't a fucking secret. Most dragons knew about them, which is why it was important to cuff him right away. No escaping. No sweet talking his way out of it.

And since they hadn't been allowed to kill dragons ever since the *Others* had organized the Big Reveal, they had no choice but to rob them blind and leave them behind.

So yeah, dragons talked like a bunch of old ladies over tea. Treasure hunters weren't *new*. But the way they had to operate within the law was.

Ugh. It was so much easier when they could just torture them for information to find the hoard. Cleanup was a lot easier too. Less risky, no loose ends to worry about.

Or at least, that's what they've heard.

"Wouldn't you like to know?" Xander drawled, lifting their gaze from their boots back to the dragon.

"I wouldn't have asked if I didn't want to know… so?"

Xander blinked at him. Was this guy for real?

Headlights splashed into the parking lot and Xander tugged off their jacket, letting the bundle rest over their cuffed hands.

"Smart," Milo mused.

Xander cut him a glare and eyed the app on their phone, confirming the make and model of the car before approaching the window. "J—"

"Jack!" Milo greeted loudly, leaning down too close into their space. "Fancy seeing you here, man."

The jovial face peered at them from the driver's seat. "Hey, not riding the bike tonight?"

"Nah. My pal here is afraid of 'em."

Xander shot him a glare filled with all the annoyance they could muster. Unfortunately, the dragon lived to laugh at whatever the driver said, and Xander grabbed the door handle.

They yanked a little too hard—

"Ow, fuck!" Milo hissed.

—and clipped Milo in the jaw.

They smiled their first genuine smile all night.

And it faded instantly as Milo tried to get in the car first out of spite. However, it was Milo's right hand that was cuffed to Xander's left. He recognized his error as his arm was pulled across his body.

"Uh, if you just go— No, the other way," Milo suggested as he tried to maneuver their arms to untangle them.

"*What* are you doing?" they hissed, exasperated as Milo waved their hands around in the air uselessly.

"Move your arm. No, twist your hand—"

They let out a frustrated grunt, yanking their arm away and shoving their head into their hands.

"Fuck!" they shouted. "Fuck," came quieter, on a frustrated breath. "Just get. Out of. The fucking. Car."

"Yep, doing that," Milo muttered, sliding out to make room for Xander.

With a huff born of too little patience for this kind of idiocy, Xander slid into the car first.

Milo dropped into his seat right after, the jacket concealing their cuffed hands from the driver.

No twisted shoulders, no crooked wrists.

"You two alright?"

"Just a bit too much to drink for this one," Xander suggested. Because it had to be the only explanation for such a dumbass.

Xander rested their hand on the seat between them, fist tightened in the material of the jacket.

It seemed Milo had the same idea, and Xander jerked their hand away from his touch as the car finally took off.

"Headed to Milo's place?" the driver asked.

"Yep," Xander said, and then rattled off the dragon's address just to make sure.

Milo snapped his head around to stare at Xander, gaze heavy with questions he couldn't—better not—ask at the moment.

That's right. I did my homework.

Pride ballooned their chest the longer Milo stared, and Xander would give anything just then to be some kind of mind reader.

It was infuriatingly entertaining to surprise the dragon. Wasn't the first time someone underestimated them. Wouldn't be the last.

But it most certainly was the first time Xander got *this* kind of rush from proving someone wrong.

3. ROLYPOLY

The treasure hunters knew his address.

Knew where he lived.

He didn't realize it at the time, but Xander had to have put it in the app to get a ride share. Why hadn't he been paying closer attention?

And why wasn't he freaking out more?

Was he so easy as to have been distracted by this human?

A rather attractive human, if you asked him.

Not that anyone had.

Sure, his dragon's scales were ruffled as fuck, pissed and pacing behind the cage of his chest at the thought of not being able to shift.

The cuff was warm around his wrist, hard and metal and engraved with runes that had to have been placed there by someone powerful, or at least someone who knew what the fuck they were doing.

Why had the hunter come to the bar? Why not just show up at his house if his house was the end game anyway? Where else would a dragon stash their hoard?

Maybe they were supposed to try seducing him. He narrowed his gaze on the headrest in front of him, then relaxed it instantly as he caught sight of himself in the rearview.

He did not look like a happy guy who was bringing a hot piece of ass home. And Jack would notice. They needed to sell it or else Jack would gossip to all his pals, and Milo would never hear the end of it.

Assuming he lived through this experience and all.

But it wasn't like he could put his arm over Xander's shoulder since they were fucking cuffed together.

I can't believe this is my life right now. This is actually happening.

He leaned over, ignoring the warning glare from Xander to place his lips by their ear.

"Try to act like you don't intend to murder me the moment we step foot in my house. Jack knows the whole town. He's a witness, a loose end. But he's just a guy. Do yourself a favor and pretend like I just whispered the sexiest thing you've ever heard in your entire life."

He paused, gave them a split second to process, and when he leaned back, he tried not to choke on his own damned breath.

Their hazel eyes were dark and half-lidded as they stared at him, heat alight in their gaze in a way that made him warm from nose to toes.

Milo leaned in, swaying toward them. Magnetized and mesmerized by the story they were telling with just that one *look.* Milo wanted to read it cover to fucking cover.

Jesus.

They blinked, a spark of irritation filtering into the warmth, shattering the intoxicating illusion. Milo leaned back, released a slow breath that was equal parts for show and equal parts because…

Because holy fucking shit, this goddamn treasure hunter had reduced him to a bag of hormones with a single *look.*

This was going to be a problem.

Gravel crunched under the tires as the car bumped over the beginning of his driveway, and Milo snapped his attention to the driver. Only a few more moments.

The car came to a stop outside his house, and to no one's surprise, Xander had nothing to say about the size of it, its location, or how fucking nice it was.

"Stalker, much?" he mumbled for their ears only as he slid out behind them. Louder, he called out to Jack, "Thanks man, have a good night."

Jack offered him a thumbs up and a wink as he drove away.

"I'm not an idiot. You think I didn't do my reconnaissance?" Xander snapped.

Milo groaned and pulled them along, leading them to the side door attached to the garage. "Watch your step," he said out of habit, manners ingrained in him from centuries ago.

As he pulled his keys out of his pocket, he froze.

Xander probably had the key on them. Why wouldn't they?

He didn't think on it long. In fact, the thought had barely crossed his mind before he dropped his own keys on the concrete and tugged his right wrist hard, the cuff biting into his skin.

Xander's eyes went wide for only a split second before they were tugged forward, and—

"Oof," Milo choked out as they tackled him to the ground, the grass softening his fall only slightly.

The cuff really got in the fucking way, but now they were face to face. Milo tried to tug his arm around, dragging Xander's left arm with him, and wrapped a hand around their slim wrist.

They huffed, sat up on their knees, and reached around their back.

Shit, they were armed to the teeth. Fucking hunters.

Milo bucked, throwing off their balance, and their hand fell away from their lower back and—

"Fuck—"

Pain, bright and loud bloomed in his nose, his sinuses stinging with the punch. The blood tickled his upper lip as it began to pour and he hissed, bucking them off again and trying to roll them over. He blocked Xander's next punch, just barely.

With his right hand, he stretched their arms up overhead, but Xander was trained for this—Milo always forgets that part—and jabbed their knee into his gut.

I fucking hate fighting.

But Milo liked his treasures, collected them for a *reason,* and he'd be damned if some stupid hunters who couldn't let go of tradition were going to take it from him.

In a last ditch effort, he rolled them over, knowing it was going to suck, knowing he was going to be sore, but at least he wouldn't be dead.

The patch of grass by the garage dropped off into an incline, and Milo let gravity do all the work for him. He pulled Xander in tight, wrapped his legs and arms around them so they couldn't move, and shoved his free hand into their back pocket.

"What the—"

No key.

Milo moved onto the next pocket, the landscape passing in a dizzying blur of darkness and trees and—hey the moon's out!—and *ouch, fuck* as Xander literally *bit* his shoulder.

He hissed a curse, but swallowed back most of the pain.

"Where's the key!" he yelled, voice taken by the wind at the speed they were rolling down the hill.

It felt like they'd been falling for hours, but in reality he knew it was only a harsh few seconds. As he checked Xander's fourth pocket, he began to lose hope.

"Where is—yes!" he shouted, felt the scrape of the rough metal against his palm. He pulled it out of their pocket, and held on tight.

"You—" Xander yelled wordlessly, bucking against him and shoving their hand between them.

A very manly shriek left Milo's lips as they twisted his nipple, and he instinctively pushed them away. The cuffs helped in no way whatsoever, and as they separated, it slowed their descent as they reached an edge.

They were airborne for only a split second, and Milo wrapped his hand tighter around the key. In the same moment, he tried to pull Xander closer, hoping to break their fall.

Humans were a lot more breakable than dragons; it was only instinct. But it was an instinct that bit him in the ass— More like, kicked him in the stomach. The air left his lungs in a whoosh, but the icing on the cake was landing on the unforgiving ground at the same time. His fist loosened and he felt the key slip from his grasp.

Gaping, trying to force air into his lungs, he saw it, watched it do a little flip in the air before splashing into the lake.

He followed right after, the shock of cold water restarting his lungs at the wrong time, and he sucked in a mouthful of murky water as the dark lake closed over his vision.

And thanks to the cuffs, where he went, so did Xander, and they splashed in alongside him.

That didn't just happen. Milo blinked beneath the water and planted his palms in the mud of the lake to push himself up before—

A hand punched into the water, fisting his shirt and hauling him up, coughing and spitting and gasping for air.

"How'd that work out for you, huh?" Xander yelled. They had a cut over their eyebrow and blood dripped down their face in a dark, sinister line in the night.

Milo was glad their question was rhetorical because he couldn't answer if he wanted to. Disbelief rattled through him and his eyes fluttered shut as he swallowed breath after breath, sitting up in the lake after Xander let him go.

Eventually, his lungs took in air on their own, and he blinked his eyes open, finding Xander, dripping and practically hissing like an angry cat. Their head was in their hands and they were shaking their head.

"I can't *believe you!*" they shouted, voice echoing off the water like a boom of thunder.

Milo crawled up on the embankment, landing with a squish. He thumped his forehead into the ground before laying his cheek on the cool grass. He dared to lift his gaze to the angry hunter beside him.

They looked absolutely furious. But beneath the anger they held onto like a shield was something Milo himself was familiar with. Something he tried never to examine too closely, something he'd worked years to overcome. But, whereas he liked to think of himself at the end of his journey, this young human looked to be in the thick of it. Shame.

"Why would you be so stupid?" they breathed, and Milo was unsure if the question was aimed at himself, or if they were speaking to their own company.

"I take it you didn't stash an extra key somewhere?" Milo asked softly.

They snapped their head up so fast Milo feared they'd given themself whiplash. And if looks could kill, Milo would be a pile of ashes.

"No. They're also enchanted, so, short of cutting off your own arm, we're not getting out of these."

Milo kept his mouth shut.

Water dripped from the wet lengths of their hair.

"What, no volunteers?" they bit out.

"What are our options?" Milo asked, keeping his voice low and even, knowing the edge he walked was made of thin ice. If he wasn't careful, Xander might just take his arm off for him.

Xander sat cross-legged in the grass, and they steepled their fingers, unconcerned that they had to drag Milo's arm across the ground to do it.

"I kill you, call in my backup, and spin a story about how your death was unavoidable. They'll bring the witch who enchanted the cuffs and undo it so I can break myself out."

"You don't seem keen on that plan," Milo observed. He wasn't stupid enough to assume it was because they'd suffer some hardship from his death. Like guilt. Xander didn't seem built for that.

Their hazel eyes flicked to him. "It's a bit too close to calling daddy for help, in my opinion."

"Any plans that don't involve killing me, maybe?"

Their gaze sharpened, but he was just glad it wasn't a knife instead.

"I would be the laughing stock of the hunters if I had to call in backup because of something like this."

Milo scoffed. "Surely it isn't the first time a key has been lost."

"First time I've heard of it," they mumbled, sounding miserable. "I can't believe this. Fuck."

As his brain turned over their options, Xander spoke again. "I need to figure this out myself. Calling them is not an option."

Milo hummed. "You're forgetting something."

"What's that?" they snapped.

"You haven't been alone in this since you locked this around my wrist," he pointed out, lifting his cuffed hand and jangling the chain. "So, as much as it pains you, you're going to have to let me help."

"I'm still waiting to hear a suggestion." Their glare was as sharp as the knives in their belt.

"I know of a witch. She's hard to find, but I bet we could do it. She'll get the cuffs off. The hunters will never have to know."

He watched the thought turn over in Xander's mind as their narrowed eyes dropped to the chain between them, brow furrowed.

Yes, there was still the issue of Xander returning without treasure. They'd have to cross that bridge when they came to it.

If they came to it.

What if, by the time they got the cuffs off, Milo could convince them *not* to rob him blind?

But how? How did Milo get past an obvious lifetime of dedication?

God, his head hurt.

"And where is this witch located?"

Milo arched a brow at them. "And reveal all my secrets? Fat chance."

Xander huffed, blowing a drop of water away from their lips and scrubbing their face with their hands in frustration. "Is it a plane ride or a car ride away?"

"Car ride. Then a hike. Maybe some climbing."

Their lips twitched. "Fine. We'll do it your way."

"Great," Milo drawled. "Can't wait to go on this adventure with you. But regardless. We aren't getting anywhere tonight with the cuffs. So we might as well..." Milo plucked at his wet shirt, wincing as it snapped back to his skin with a wet plop. "Clean up. Sleep."

"Sleep? You think I can sleep knowing you're inches away from me?"

"You wound me," Milo drawled, rubbing at the uncomfortable tightness in his chest.

Xander didn't have to know he wasn't being sarcastic when he said it.

"I'll sleep just fine. What you do is your own business. Now come on, it's fucking cold out here and I need a shower." He tugged on their chained hands.

Milo practically *heard* their temper rise, was slightly surprised there wasn't steam coming out of their ears as he glanced back at their choked off noise.

"I'm not showering with you!" they snapped, cheeks red, visible even in the dim light of the waning moon.

Milo would bet one of his pretty trinkets they hated blushing. "Well, listen. I am not sleeping smelling like... *this.* So you either magically take the cuffs off me, or you stand outside the fucking shower while I wash the lake out of my *hair.*"

"I don't have the key, asshole," they snarled, taking a step closer.

Milo stared at them, gaze darting between their eyes, studying them for the tiniest sign of give. There was none.

"Guess there's only one option then," Milo announced.

4. STUPID PLOY

"I will make you sleep outside. I'm not getting offed in the shower by some treasure hunter."

They blinked.

Xander probably would've argued. Would've snapped back something ultimately cutting, really dug deep.

Instead, their mind stumbled over the phrase *getting off* and latched onto *shower*.

And Milo *was* already soaking wet and dripping on his nice hardwood floor, shirt sticking to him like a second skin and outlining his strong, lean frame and his stupid biceps and his *pecs*. God, why?

Why was this dragon so hot? Just to torture Xander?

Xander schooled their expression, and removed their sopping wet gloves before once again tugging off their coat.

There was just one problem.

"How are we going to get this off?" they asked, letting the coat sleeve slip down their arm to dangle over the cuffs, further leaking onto the dragon's floor.

They tried not to smile as Milo caught it, and huffed under its weight. "Jesus, what's in this thing?"

"Weapons," they answered simply. Then cocked their head to the side as they considered something else entirely.

"As a matter of fact, how are you going to get your shirt off?" How would Xander take theirs off?

Milo glanced down at his chest as if he'd forgotten what he was wearing. How infuriatingly adorable was that?

"We'll cross that bridge when we come to it. Weapons."

Xander tried not to feel embarrassed about Milo's more than obvious stare as they unbuckled their harness and holsters, letting them fall to the table with a clatter. With a glare, Xander tugged the knife from the sheath at the small of their back and tossed it in the pile. Followed by the one at their hip.

Then the smaller throwing daggers from their pocket.

Then they had to undo the buckles of the thigh harness and remove the knives from those holsters under his watchful gaze.

The one tucked in their calf.

And of course, couldn't forget the boot dagger.

"Are you fucking done?" Milo grumbled.

Xander glared at him, narrowing their eyes before finally huffing and lifting their shirt.

"Jesus, really?" Milo whined. *Whined.*

Unfortunately, it was just as sexy as it sounded, even drenched in annoyance, but Xander ignored it like the strong individual they were trained to be and removed their last dagger.

Milo turned his back and began walking, and Xander had to make quick work of the belt around their waist before letting it drop to the ground. At the sound, Milo spun, glare sliding away into slack surprise.

"A *whip*? Really? Are you fucking Indiana Jones?"

Xander blinked innocently, deciding that ruffling this dragon's scales was their new mission in life. "I can't say I have, no."

Milo cocked his head, reexamining his words before huffing. "You—" he seemed to think better of whatever response was on the tip of his tongue. "Come on," he urged, and tugged them along.

Following behind Milo, Xander let their gaze drift around his house. Past the double doors that concealed the living room, parlor, whatever rich people called them. Everything was dark and moody, but still cozy, with trinkets and art and random other shit hanging on the walls. More wall was covered than was bare, and Xander's eyes widened as they passed a shelving compartment on the wall, tiny, shiny rocks within each little cubby.

There were even sconces, which was ridiculous in this day and age. Each of the rooms they passed—Jesus, how many rooms did one dragon need—was equally as decorated.

Was that a *theater*?

The bedroom Milo finally led them to was much the same. Dark, warm colors and more framed art and trinkets lining the walls.

They pointedly avoided looking at the bed.

"Well, we're here. Crossing this bridge. Now what?" Xander drawled.

The low lights shimmered around them, making the remaining water on Milo's bare chest glisten in a most unfair fashion.

He removed his shirt, peeled it off until it was dangling from their chains by one sleeve, along with Xander's jacket.

Xander liked that jacket. It was one of their favorites. They'd had it for a while—longer than they could remember —but it'd held up nice and it had all their favorite secret pockets for weapons.

"How are we gonna get dressed after the shower? These cuffs are really a pain in the ass," Milo grouched, shooting them a less than favorable glare.

"Oh, I'm sorry, was I the one who attacked you and lost

the key?" they snapped. Milo's glare softened the more they talked, and by the time the last word skated past their lips, he looked too close to hurt for comfort. Xander sighed. "Do you own a poncho? Or shawls? Anything without sleeves?"

His brows lifted, eyes sparkling, and he framed Xander's shoulders with his warm palms. "Yes! I do! That's genius!"

Xander blinked as he gave them a little shake of excitement. "Come with me."

"As if I have a choice?" they called after him. Milo was already dragging them through a doorway and into a walk-in closet. Xander tried their hardest not to stare at the way the muscles in his back moved as he walked. Most noticeable were the scales that, even with the shift-locking cuffs, shimmered beneath the lighting. They lined the back of his shoulders, crawled up beneath the long curls of his hair. How far up his neck did they go?

Xander's eyes widened as they entered the closet, row after row of clothes and shoes filling the room. Some of them were modern tee shirts and jeans, but some looked straight out of a history book. They lifted their hand to feel a pair of shiny trousers. "All of this is *yours*?"

"Well, when you've lived as long as I have, you tend to collect quite a few things. Including..." he muttered to himself for a moment as he tossed hangers back and forth on the rack. "A ha! Here," he said absently, tossing a bundle of fabric over his shoulder.

Xander caught it, eyes slightly widening at the silky softness of it.

"This wouldn't protect against rain. Or any element, for that matter," they mused aloud.

Milo turned with his own poncho and shrugged. "No, but tell me that isn't a great fabric. Soft as hell."

The dragon led them from the closet, and Xander called

after him, "Let me get this straight. You own not one, but *two* useless ponchos just because they feel nice?"

Milo glanced over his shoulder, confusion clear on his face. "More than two, actually. That a problem?"

"No, it's just fuckin' weird. And a waste of money," they muttered. There's no way a fabric this nice was cheap.

"My money. My ponchos," he called in a sing-song voice.

God, dragons were weird.

Their eyes widened.

If his closet was filled with things *this* nice, what must this dragon have in his hoard?

Shit.

Distracted imagining the shiniest of gems and even nicer fabrics, pretty baubles and bells and whistles, they failed to realize that Milo had stopped, and bumped into his back.

"Sorry," they muttered, jumping back as far as the chain would let them.

"No worries. I don't bite," Milo said.

Of course he couldn't bite. He couldn't shift. Xander cocked their head to the side.

"O-kay then. Now… shit. Having claws right now would be so nice," he grumbled, tugging at the shirt still dangling from the cuffs.

Xander sighed, reached into one of the secret jacket pockets, and pulled out a blade. Before Milo could protest about hiding weapons, they held up his shirt and sliced it through the sleeve, letting it fall free to flutter to the floor.

"Hey! You could have at least cut along the seam so I could repair that."

Their lips parted slightly. That was a good idea.

When it came to their own jacket, Xander dug the knife in and carefully sliced it along the seam. "Smart," they muttered.

"Oh, I see, save your jacket but fuck my shirt, right?"

"Once again, couldn't read your mind. Should have spoken up sooner."

"You could've *told* me what you were planning—" Milo cut himself off with a deep, put-upon sigh. "It doesn't matter. I just want to shower."

Their jacket flopped to the floor about the same time Milo's pants did, and Xander turned their back, cheeks flaming.

"A warning, please!" Xander snapped.

Milo only chuckled, and annoyance flushed through Xander anew.

With their arm stretched out behind them, they had to walk backward as Milo made his way to the shower. The curtain rustled as Milo got in, and the shower turned on.

I can't believe this is happening.

Xander *seethed.*

As the shower rained down on Milo, who began humming an annoying tune behind the curtain, Xander thought of every way they'd enjoy killing him.

Each time their hand got wet from being dragged under the spray as Milo washed his *precious* hair, Xander ground their teeth together.

They could choke him out with the chain, maybe snap his neck or something. In theory.

Stabbing. Been there, done that. Xander was *very* experienced in that field.

"If you're thinking about killing me, just remember *I* know where the witch is. And you'd have to drag my body around for like, ever. Unless you want the hunters' help, of course."

At the pointed reminder, Xander ground their teeth together. "I know all of this," Xander bit out.

"Just reminding you. I can practically hear you plotting over there."

Xander didn't respond, and Milo went back to humming. *"I'm not getting offed in the shower by some treasure hunter."*

Too bad Xander's own brain was betraying them. Replaying Milo's stupid words, grumbled in that stupidly low voice he'd used.

He was probably doing it on purpose. Trying to throw Xander off their game. Distract them.

Their eyes snapped open.

Yes. This was all a stupid ploy.

Slutty fucking dragons.

Milo was trying to seduce them! Get them to lower their inhibitions.

Hmph. They'd show him.

Xander was infallible. Unseducable.

They frowned, then instantly snapped their eyes shut again as the curtain shifted, a line of warm, tan skin coming into sight a split second before they shut it out.

Shirtless.

What? No.

No, no.

Removing clothes wasn't necessary for smothering. Or maiming.

Yes, maiming would do.

It was a long moment before the shower shut off, steam filling the room. A line of lake water trailed down Xander's spine, and they huffed as a hand appeared around the shower curtain. "Towel, please?"

Xander actually growled, but ultimately handed him the towel off the rack.

A long moment passed, and Xander heard every swipe of the cloth against his skin, collecting the water drops that were no doubt caressing him, glimmering in the low light cast by the shadow of the curtain.

"Your turn," he announced, pulling the curtain back with

a dramatic swish. The towel was wrapped around his hips, and Xander tried *very* hard not to let their gaze wander. It was hard to ignore the shiny red scales that lined his stomach, leading down to the towel.

Like a good little hunter, they kept their gaze above the waist. To save themself the embarrassment, they stepped over the lip of the tub into the shower and pulled the curtain behind them.

They took a deep breath, making sure there were no dragons peeking through the curtain before fussing to get their shirt off. It was one they were less attached to, so they didn't bother finding the right seam before they sliced it through.

They folded what they could of the shirt, and carefully stripped off their wet pants, managing to do it without falling out of the tub. The knife they pulled from the pocket went on the shelf inset into the shower wall. Just in case.

Next were their boxer briefs, and with it came the packer, which they suddenly wished they'd left behind for this mission.

But it wasn't like they could foresee this unfortunate set of circumstances. They felt *very* exposed in the moment, and cursed their luck again before folding the clothes around the fake, flesh-colored cock. The chain clanked against the side of the tub as they squatted down to lower the pile of clothes to the ground.

That didn't work, so instead they reached out and balanced it on the lid of the toilet, making sure it wouldn't fall. With a quick glance, they confirmed that Milo was turned away, dressed in his stupid silky poncho.

At least he was being polite, not being a creep. They didn't want to have to put the knife to use.

As they started the shower, they waited for Milo to make some smartass comment.

However, there was only silence on the other side of the curtain, and Xander yanked the knob to turn the water hotter before either of them could say anything.

The poncho would have to do until they found the witch.

They turned their face up to the spray and let it wash the flush from their cheeks. As the murk from the grassy cliffside went down the drain, so too did Xander's emotional distress about the unfortunate circumstances. They'd never done something so embarrassing and *stupid*, moving too early. If only they'd waited, cuffed Milo after he'd brought them back to his place.

They gripped the ring hanging from their neck, reminded themself what was at stake here, and hardened their resolve.

"Don't freak out," Milo said, as the chain suddenly went limp. "I'm tired of holding my arm out, so I'm gonna sit on the—"

Xander *heard* the flop of something heavy and rubber land on the ground, and their mouth dropped open.

They stared down at the drain, silently wishing it would swallow them up along with the hot water.

"Did you... lose something?" Milo asked, voice carefully controlled.

Xander stuck their head under the water, wondering if Milo would let them waterboard themself instead of having to face him again.

No. We can be cool about this. It happens. It's fine.

They stuck their hand out the shower curtain, mumbling a sharp, "Towel."

The fabric hit their palm and Milo wisely didn't say anything else, and as the moment stretched on, the bathroom silent as they dried themself, they sighed.

"Like I said, I'm non-binary. I prefer using they and them pronouns."

"That's cool," Milo said simply. "Ready for the poncho?" he asked.

And that was… it?

They held the towel back out once they were dry, and Milo exchanged it for the poncho.

"Should I pick it up or—"

"*Don't* touch it," Xander shouted in their haste, yanking open the curtain, but making sure it covered their body. "Leave it alone. I'll get it."

Milo's lips twitched as he lifted his hands in innocence. "Got it. No touching."

With a glare, Xander snapped the curtain back in place and repeated every curse they'd ever heard in their life.

The soft fabric of the poncho startled Xander at first, having already forgotten its comfort. They shivered as they pulled it overhead and tugged at the hem, thankful it at least covered them to their knees.

"Oh, uh… I can get you a pair of boxers too, but uh, it requires both of us," Milo said, jangling the chain.

"Yeah, yeah," Xander said, and tugged the curtain aside to step out, knife in hand and still considering using it.

Milo narrowed his gaze. "I know you know how stupid it would be to stab me, so I'll let you keep that. Try to refrain from killing me in my sleep. It'd be *really* unfortunate."

Xander mumbled a noncommital answer, if only for the joy of seeing Milo's eyes narrow in worry.

Xander bent down, the poncho pooling around them in a surprisingly thorough cover. "I can still kick your ass," Xander added as they snatched the packer up before folding it back in their clothes.

"Oh, I don't doubt that," Milo grumbled, and kindly kept his eyes averted while Xander situated their pile.

"I don't have any pants that would fit you, I don't think.

And the boxers might be loose, but they'll work," he rambled, and Xander finally followed him into the bedroom.

Milo led them to a chest of drawers along the wall opposite the bed, digging through it loudly.

Eventually, he dangled a pair out to them, and Xander snatched them with a sigh. "Turn around," they urged.

Milo did so without arguing.

Good. Maybe they'd scared him into cooperation. One could hope, even after they'd fucked up the mission so royally.

It shouldn't matter what a stupid dragon thought of them.

It really shouldn't.

But somehow, it did.

5. MORNING COFFEE

Xander was *so* comfortable.

Like, more comfortable than they'd ever been.

That should've been warning enough, and yet sleep, her deft, warm fingers held them captive, and Xander couldn't be convinced to fight her. Rain pattered outside the window, and Xander was overwhelmed with the *coziness* of the moment.

But slowly, despite their determination to hold onto the soft dream of soft things, reality intervened. The previous day returned to them in flashes, and their eyes snapped open to…

A warm chest beneath their cheek, sleep-deep breaths lifting and lowering them gently.

A very *bare* chest.

Xander pressed up in a rush, scrambling away from the dragon with a huff and a decidedly undignified bark. In their panic, the cuff didn't register until they landed on the floor with a grunt, arm outstretched toward the bed, where the other half of their problem blinked blearily down at them.

"I was just rudely pulled from my slumber, so forgive me, but what the fuck?" Milo rasped.

Xander stared up at him, trying to will away the redness heating their cheeks. "I— Uh..."

"What are you on the floor for?" he interrupted.

"Bad dream?" Xander said, though it spilled out in a question.

Milo hummed, and then promptly rolled over. "Whatever crisis you're having can wait until I get a few more hours of sleep."

"Hours! It's already..." they trailed off, searching for a clock, any clock, and finally found an ancient analog clock on the wall across the room. "It's eight AM," they argued.

"Too early," Milo grumbled, and tugged on the chain connecting them.

"It's—"

"Shh. That's enough noise for now."

Xander's mouth dropped open, and they sat up, *just* able to see Milo pretending to be asleep.

Who slept in this late? Eight in the morning is a perfectly reasonable time to start the day!

While Xander's internal thoughts ran rampant, they climbed back up on the bed and re-situated their position *out* of Milo's reach.

Xander didn't know who reached for whom in the night, and they supposed it didn't matter. What mattered was that Milo hadn't caught them, and therefore didn't have more ammo to hold over Xander's head.

Xander, however, would take the secret to their *grave.* No one had to know that they cuddled a dragon.

Their eyes shuttered in horror. A treasure hunter cuddling a dragon. Who'd heard of such a thing?

Milo twitched in his sleep, and Xander rolled their head to the side to glare at his offensive existence.

Really? Why wouldn't he have kept the poncho on? Why?

It was cosmically unfair how attractive the man was, and at this point he was just dangling it in front of Xander.

But… they supposed they understood why he wasn't in his poncho. As soft as it was, the damned thing was twisted around them every which way. The front half was stuck beneath them while the back half was still spilled over the side of the bed from their tumble.

Milo slept soundly beside them, his breaths having evened out while Xander lay still, glaring at the ceiling. They supposed they could rustle around and fix the damned thing, but that was certain to wake up Milo, and wasn't there a saying about waking a sleeping beast?

On a normal day, they'd have already awoken and called in a progress report to their supervisor, but their phone was on the table with the weapons and—

Their eyes widened. If they didn't check in… would the hunters get worried? Send in backup without asking?

Fuck.

Consequences be damned, they lifted their chained hand and pushed at Milo's shoulder. "Milo. I need to check in with my supervisor. I need my phone."

He rumbled some kind of sleep drenched noise that was absolutely untranslatable before he went quiet.

They tried again. "Wake up," they hissed. "Come with me to get my phone and then you can go back to sleep."

Milo straight up ignored them that time, or he didn't care. Xander couldn't tell which one it was, and huffed before falling back to the mattress with a huff. Arthur trusted them. He wouldn't send in reinforcements without at least touching base.

They'd spent a long time earning his trust. A lifetime, some might argue. He knew how capable Xander was, had no reason to doubt them. Getting to the phone was something that could wait a few more hours.

It wasn't like they were likely to drag Milo through the house, and besides, Arthur would probably ask questions that Xander didn't want to answer in front of Milo. And with the way they were connected, it was unavoidable, at least for the moment.

They'd have to wait until they found a way to get the cuffs removed. *Then* they could call in with an update.

In the meantime, Xander would have to find a way to gain access to Milo's hoard. No matter what the dragon claimed, hoards *always* had something of value in them. Xander had yet to come across one that didn't.

But how? How would they convince Milo to give it up? Their leverage was in the bottom of his fucking lake.

As they lay awake plotting, planning, hoping, the rain gave way to a dreary, overcast morning.

It made the light in the room a soft, cozy gray, and yet Milo was no less bright because of it. Damned dragon.

Xander rolled over to glare at him some more.

Stupid curls. Dumb full lips and his square, speckled jaw. And those *lashes*. Was this guy real?

Xander was *not* checking him out. Nope… But they did roll back over and glare at the ceiling about it instead of at the dragon himself. It was just past ten when Milo finally stirred again, stretching obnoxiously with a loud yawn.

Xander yanked their hand back from where Milo had dragged it up the bed with his own.

"Did someone wake up on the wrong side of the bed this morning?" Milo asked, voice still raspy from sleep, but his gaze was more alert.

Grinding their teeth together, Xander sat up and finally adjusted the fucking poncho so it wasn't twisted around their torso. "Finally. Can we get going now? The sooner we find this witch you claim to know, the sooner we can get out of these cuffs."

"Sheesh, can't a dragon get a cup of coffee? I just woke up, you know," he replied far too casually for their liking.

"Oh, I *know*," they practically growled.

"Fine, fine. Where's my poncho?" he murmured distractedly, gaze already bouncing around the room. As he stood up to dress, Xander had to crawl across the bed after him, swallowing down their temper the entire way.

In the kitchen, Milo piddled around while Xander flipped through their phone, frowning at the lack of messages. On the off chance Arthur had already sent hunters their way, Xander shot off a text briefly explaining that they needed more time. It was read immediately, but no response came thereafter.

They frowned, but ultimately locked the phone and slid it into their pocket.

"Brace yourself," Milo hummed, and then the deafening whir of the coffee bean grinder filled the kitchen. It was over as quickly as it had started, and the scent of rich coffee permeated the air.

Xander had to follow Milo around the kitchen like a puppy, gritting their teeth the whole time as Milo went about his morning routine. They ignored him by studying the kitchen more closely. Colorful mixing bowls were stacked on the counter, clean but chipped from use. The apron hanging on the hook by the entrance was stained and dusted with flour.

They glanced around the decor on the walls, the used kitchen utensils sitting in a bowl by the stove.

Tidy. Neat. Well used.

"Is this what you do every day?" they bit out. This dragon's life was so comfortable. Peaceful. Baking fucking cakes and whatnot.

"Today is more lax than most, I suppose. Since I can't go into the bakery and all," he answered, jangling their chain as if Xander had forgotten its existence in the past five minutes.

Spoiler alert: They hadn't.

"I'm usually up by three or four, readying to go in and get the goods started before the shop opens. I don't always sleep in," he said, leaning back against the counter, long hair curling above his shoulders in an absolutely sinful manner.

Xander leaned against the bar behind them, arms crossed and chain stretched between them.

The coffee steamed and dripped in the background, and Xander had absolutely never had coffee that smelled so delicious.

"So where is this witch you know?" Xander asked, turning the subject from less personal matters.

"It's been a long time since I've been out there, and I usually fly. Haven't ever hiked there, but I'd say we'll be in for a few hours. Hope you didn't have any other plans today." His lips twitched, lifting up at one corner with no idea how devastating it was to Xander, the fucker.

"Better not get us lost," they bit out, refusing to give anything away.

A beep chimed behind Milo and he turned, busying himself with his coffee while Xander waited. They drummed their fingers along the tabletop just to be annoying.

"Here," Milo said, and turned, holding out a steaming cup of coffee.

Xander's lips parted slightly in surprise, and instinctively their hands came up to take the mug from the dragon.

It warmed their hands, and their gaze flicked to the dragon's over the lip of the mug, through the steam of the coffee. The scent tickled their nose in the best way, a deep, rich scent taking up arms against the dreary clouds outside.

"Thanks," they offered.

Milo hummed, that smirk still in place as he watched

Xander flounder at the kindness. It was just a cup of coffee for fuck's sake, and they did their best to shake off whatever emotions were bubbling to the surface.

"Not very poncho weather," Milo mused as he glanced over Xander's shoulder, out the window across the room.

"Not these at least," Xander agreed, keeping their gaze locked on the rain slick panes over his shoulder.

"Yes, yes, we've covered that I shop not for utility, but for pleasure. Imagine that."

God, his voice. It was so unfair the way it slid out warm as the coffee and rich as the scent of it.

Xander lifted the cup to their lips if only to have something else to focus on. It spilled over their tongue, nutty and bitter and rich and the best fucking coffee they'd ever had. Was that cinnamon?

Unbidden, a hum slipped out. Once they realized, their eyes snapped open—when exactly had they drifted closed— to find Milo looking rather proud of himself.

Something else, too, lurked in the depths of his eyes, but Xander wasn't ready to explore that yet. Or ever! Never.

"I sprinkle cinnamon over the beans before I brew it."

"It's nice," Xander decided to reveal. Better than the *lovely, divine, delicious,* that crossed their mind.

"Mhm," Milo hummed as if he could read their mind, and they narrowed their gaze before taking another sip. The taste alone eased their glare.

They drank their coffee in silence, barely more than a foot apart, Milo's kitchen seeming smaller with every passing moment. Xander kept their gaze fixed on the window, watching the rain taper off before calling it quits completely. All that remained were the clouds and the humidity.

Milo's gaze still boring into them yet giving nothing away.

Xander cleared their throat.

"Ready to get started, then?"

6. SCALES

Milo was dying.

Not to be dramatic.

Xander, standing in his kitchen, softer than he'd ever seen them—as if he'd known them more than a handful of hours—was killing him.

Barefoot and free of weapons, hair still tousled from sleep. Their little fall out of the bed. The cuddle they most likely didn't want him to remember.

But oh, he likely wouldn't be forgetting their weight against him anytime soon.

They liked his coffee. Liked his ponchos, despite their uselessness.

What else would they like?

Milo couldn't afford thoughts like these, but like with everything else in life, he indulged.

They were a treasure hunter. A dragon hunter. Had probably taken their fair share of scales and stolen hoards and many other things less savory. But Milo couldn't find it in himself to care about anything that happened, anything they'd done prior to Xander stepping over the threshold of his home.

It was intimate, this moment they shared over brewed

coffee on a rainy morning with responsibilities hoisted above both their heads, waiting to drop like an anvil in a cheesy cartoon.

And yet, Milo could still sense Xander wished to be anywhere but here. Were they still embarrassed about what happened in the bathroom? Milo wanted to say something to reassure them, but any kind of assurance from Milo was likely unwelcome. Still, it was no worse than that one time Milo left a dildo on the counter while the plumber had to come do some work. Shit happened.

Or maybe it was simply their sense of responsibility that demanded they feel that way, and had yet to learn how to fight it.

"Ready to get started then?" Xander asked.

"Yes, I certainly feel more human now," Milo mused.

It was the wrong thing to say, to remind them that Milo was anything *but* human. They held out their empty mug, expression shuttered once again.

"Then what are we waiting on?"

That was the question, wasn't it?

With the moment ruined, Milo finished his morning routine while playing a pretty decent host, if you asked him.

Again, not that anyone had.

But he fished out a new spare toothbrush for the *guest,* and even waited patiently while they strapped on all their harnesses and holsters and collected their weapons and slid their gloves deftly over their slim fingers.

God, why me?

"She's a witch, not a pack of wolves," Milo muttered, distracted by the way Xander tightened their thigh harness.

Life was so unfair.

"You never know. Better to be overprepared than underprepared."

"And what if they turn us away because you look too threatening?"

"Me?" they asked in surprise and then drifted their gaze over Milo. "No, you're right, I *would* be the threatening one. You look like a puppy."

Milo chose not to take offense at that, and shifted his hand in the air between them. "My point exactly. Couldn't you take just a few less knives?"

"No," Xander answered dryly. "Any other questions?"

Milo snagged his keys from the hook by the door. "I suppose not. Let's go."

Xander led him out the door and into the disgustingly warm, humid air.

It was truly unfair how good they looked, even strapped to the nines with their weapons. Maybe especially because of them.

Milo opened the driver side door and motioned for Xander to climb in, not wanting another tangled, embarrassing mess like the night before. This time was certainly less chaotic, and Xander slid into the bucket seats with ease.

The car purred to life after he slid into his own seat and rested his hand on the gear shift so as not to strain the chain between them.

It rattled as they went over a few bumps, a bit of gravel unearthed from its place in the overnight storm.

It was quiet. Too quiet. Xander clearly wasn't one to lead a conversation, and Milo couldn't come up with something, anything to talk about. The chances of Xander reciprocating were slim to none, anyway.

So the drive went slow. Into the mountains and through the winding roads, past turnoff after turnoff until the trails became less common and the signs grew more weathered, if not outright decayed.

"Are you sure you know where you're going?" Xander questioned.

He slowed the car, taking a sharp curve carefully before he spied the grown over pathway he was searching for.

"There," he said, and directed the car onto a wet patch of grass. If he was lucky, it wouldn't be stuck in the mud by the time they returned.

They exited the car the same way they entered, awkwardly and one at a time, Xander carefully stepping over the console and only getting a little mud in his leather seat.

With a sigh, he decided he'd deal with that later.

Xander was vibrating with nerves—urgency maybe—and Milo figured they better find the witches sooner rather than later.

"No map or anything?" Xander accused. "You're just raw dogging it?"

Milo choked on a laugh. "I have a pretty good memory. So yes, I'm raw dogging it."

"If you get me lost in here, I swear—"

Milo hummed. "What, you'll stab me and then drag around my dead body and hope the witches find *you* instead?"

They glared at him. "Not every hit is a kill hit. I could maim you."

"Maim, huh? What would you do, take off a pinky?"

"I think I'd start with your fucking hand so I can finally get these damned cuffs off!"

Milo turned away and headed into the forest before they could see his smile twitch. Something told him Xander wouldn't take well to being riled up on purpose.

But, oh, was it fun.

He'd had safer pastimes, though.

With a huff, and no choice, Xander followed after him.

"I'm glad you wore boots," Milo mused aloud as the soft ground gave way beneath his steps.

"Always be prepared," Xander reminded him of their earlier words, and he rolled his eyes.

"Yeah, yeah."

It was slow going at first. The trail was mostly grown up, but they could make out just enough to stay on track. The further in they got, the harder it became, until they couldn't tell the trail apart at all. The sun stretched overhead, making it warm and humid beneath the overgrown trees.

"Guess we're on our own now."

"*Don't* get us lost," Xander warned.

"You have no faith in me at all," Milo accused.

"Damn right I don't."

With a sigh, Milo shook his head. "Shouldn't I be the one with no faith? You know where I live. It would be nothing for you just to kill me, take my car, and find the hoard in my house."

"Don't tempt me." Xander's voice dripped with sarcasm.

Silence fell again, and Milo felt no better than he had at the start of all this. "Wanna play twenty questions?" he tried again after helping Xander stretch across a ravine.

They took their hand back as if his touch offended them, and he ignored the sting in his chest.

"Sure, I'll start. Do all dragons talk this much?" they asked, tone absolutely cutting.

What did it say about him that it only encouraged Milo?

"I think I can safely say each dragon is different. Haven't you met a few, being a dragon hunter and all?"

They turned a frown in his direction. "I'm a treasure hunter, not a dragon hunter."

"You're telling me there's a difference?"

"Do you really wanna know the answer to that?"

Was Milo going to get a truthful answer? Did it matter what they'd done in their past?

"I asked if you'd met them, not killed them," Milo directed the conversation in a safer manner.

"I've met quite a few dragons. Never talked to one quite as long as I have you, though."

"Don't make this cuffing thing a habit then?"

"The rules changed after the Big Reveal," they admitted with a huff. "Hell of a lot more complicated now."

"Why? Because you can't outright kill us anymore?" It slipped out before he could stop himself, but the question didn't seem to phase Xander.

"We have to be more careful now. When *Others* were still a secret, it was easier to operate outside the law. Now though, we're all the same. We'd answer for the death of an Other just like we would a human."

"So, in other words, yes."

Xander glanced over at him again, expression carefully neutral. "In other words, yes."

"Now you're having to get more creative," he guessed, jangling the chain.

"Not very successfully, if you ask me," they muttered. "My turn. Where's your hoard?"

"Good one," Milo offered with a grin. "Pass."

"What's the most valuable item you own?"

Milo mulled over the question, imagining his own hoard at home. "I guess you could consider my car. I'm kind of hurt you didn't even comment on it."

"I'm not a car person," Xander said. "What is it?"

"Hello? A Maserati Sebring. How can you not appreciate it? It's in mint condition. It's *red* interior. I traded it off some guy."

"What'd you trade, if it's so fancy?"

"A few dragon scales."

That pulled Xander to a stop. "A *few*?"

"Oh, don't be so dramatic. I lost them during shedding season so they weren't as in good condition as they are when they're... you know, ripped out of the skin."

Xander frowned. "It hurts?"

Milo didn't know whether to find comfort in the fact that Xander didn't know, or horror in the idea that they hadn't cared. Treasure hunter's greatest hauls were scales.

"Our scales are sacred. Like fingerprints, they're all individual. The patterns, colors, swirls, arrangements all differ from dragon to dragon. That's why they go for so much on the market. But you know this already," he murmured, keeping pace with them and shoving a branch out of the way.

"You're right. I do know all that. Didn't know it hurt though." They frowned.

He came to a stop, reached out for Xander's slim fingers, held their hand out between them. Their gaze widened at the proximity, but Milo gave no quarter. He spread their palm wide open. "Scales are big. You know this, too. About this size, actually." His voice was soft as he traced a circle in their palm, studying their expression while he spoke. Their gaze was locked on where they touched. "Imagine taking one of those *very* sharp knives you carry and slicing a piece of your skin off about that big."

Their eyes widened.

"That's what plucking a scale feels like. Being skinned alive, piece by piece. That's why dragons hate hunters." He dropped their hand and continued forward, more than a little surprised by the anger that spread through his chest.

Xander's steps were fucking silent as they trailed alongside him, and Milo cursed every snapped twig, every crunch of a dead leaf beneath his own feet. *How* did they do that?

"How long have you been a hunter?"

Xander cleared their throat. "Almost fifteen years."

His eyes widened. "How is that possible? You can't be a day over twenty-five."

"Flattery will get you nowhere. I'm almost thirty," they admitted.

"Do they recruit from the fucking cradle now?" he hissed.

"I was… a special case," they finally said. "My… supervisor took me in."

"That's not even fucking legal, is it?" Milo asked, eyes wide. This was the twenty-first century, you couldn't just pick up a kid off the streets.

Xander arched a brow at him. "Hunters are efficient. Know what they're doing, and are connected to the right people. He made it legal."

Milo wished he could see what was going through their mind at this moment. He could only imagine the worst things, cruel training, propaganda, taught and manipulated from such a young age.

Did Xander even recognize how wrong that was?

"I know it's fucked up, but it's all I've known, and I'm mostly on my own now. S'not so bad."

Milo reeled while they came to another dried up ravine, a tree having fallen and providing a natural bridge.

A slippery death trap is what it was.

"Be careful," he warned.

But he should've known, it wasn't Xander he had to worry about. Their footing was sure and certainly more secure than his own.

It wasn't fair, is what it was. He was a fucking dragon, could glide through the air effortlessly and faster than he'd ever maintained even in his fancy car. And he couldn't even walk across a fucking bridge without—

"Will you hurry up?" Xander snapped. "At this rate, it'll be dark before we fucking get there."

Milo snapped his head up from glaring down at his own

feet. "I'm sorry, I don't often spend my time traversing slippery, moss ridden logs of wood in the forest."

"You're making *me* nervous. Just walk!"

Despite the sharp prick of his irritation, he listened to them and just… walked. Avoided the leaves just begging for a slip, and made it to the other side unscathed.

"Does Princess need a hand?" Xander asked after they hopped off the log, turning and walking away without actually offering a hand.

Milo rolled his eyes and made it to the ground without error.

Next was a fallen tree, the damned thing almost coming to his waist. Xander cleared it with no issue, and as they straddled the log, for the first time, Milo noticed a ring dangling from a leather cord around their neck.

His stomach pitched south. Was it a wedding ring? Was Xander fucking *married*? Or worse, what if they were widowed?

The question itched to scratch past his lips, but he held it back. They tucked the ring back in the neck of the poncho and waited patiently for Milo to climb over the tree.

"You've gotta be fucking kidding me," Xander muttered, and Milo turned at once to the forest before them.

"Oh no," Milo groaned.

What he'd give to be a dragon right now, able to fly them to the top. Right to the witch's front door.

A giant boulder blocked their path a few yards ahead, split down the middle, covered in moss and leaves, and slick from the storm.

"How are we supposed to get over *that*?" Milo groaned.

Xander grunted, the sound long and drawn out and filled with the same frustration that laced Milo's thoughts.

"This cannot get any worse," they muttered.

Milo snapped his head to them, a glare already on his

features and lips twisted in a snarl. He was interrupted by the boom of thunder that shot through the sky like a cannonball, followed by the first drops of rain.

"Wanna try that again?" Milo groused.

Xander's eyes fluttered shut out of pure disbelief, and suddenly Milo couldn't help himself. A chuckle bubbled over, spilled out just as the downpour began. His chuckles were lost in the sudden roar of rain, the thin ponchos soaking through almost instantly.

"What's so fucking funny?" Xander yelled.

Milo shook his head and continued forward. Sure, they could attempt to walk around it. If they wanted to have a repeat of the other night by tipping down the mountainside. Nor could they scale the incline on the opposite direction. The rock was blocking their only way forward.

So, boulder it was.

It wasn't a smooth boulder, so surely they could find some footing.

"Rather conveniently placed, isnt it?" Xander asked, blinking against the downpour.

"Can't get anything past you," Milo shouted.

Xander came to a stop. "So this is the witch's doing?"

"I would assume so. What better way to protect your home than to make it impossible to get to?"

"Going through an awful lot of trouble to keep anyone away. Do you think she'll even help us?"

"Only one way to find out."

Milo stared up at the cracked and broken piece. It would make a good start, elevate them enough to maybe reach the rest of the boulder.

"Well, come on," Milo urged, and curled his hands around the jagged piece above his head.

It took some maneuvering to get the momentum he needed, but eventually he curled his ankle around the lip and pulled himself up. Laying flat, he stretched his right hand down, chain dangling down to Xander, who stared up at him with slightly parted lips.

God, what he'd give to know what was going through their mind at the moment. Hopefully, they were appreciating the prime example of his magnificent form.

Xander blinked up at him, rain splattering against their face and flattening their hair across their forehead.

Instead of taking the offered hand, they repeated much the same move that Milo did, but with a little more dignity.

"Now you're just showing off," Milo said as they pulled themself up. The poncho was slick against their skin, displaying the muscles of their upper arms.

"So what if I am?" Xander retorted, crawling onto the crooked rock surface and balancing beside Milo. They tilted their head back and Milo had to physically pry his head in the same direction, far too enamored by the long line of their throat.

"How are we supposed to get all the way up there?"

"Very carefully," Milo answered, and stood, planting his feet precariously and waiting for Xander to join him.

"I know you're very strong and impressive," Milo began, yelling over the crash of the rain around them. "But do you think you'd consider letting me hoist you up there?"

Their brows knotted in the middle as they glanced from the tip of the boulder before them, and back to Milo. "Fine. Don't fucking drop me!"

"Wouldn't dream of it," Milo returned.

They probably maybe could've scaled it, but then Milo wouldn't have the chance to wrap his hands around Xander's waist.

They were so much larger than life in skill and attitude and fortitude, he was actually surprised by how far his hands went around them, spare inches from touching.

His fantasy was ruined by the sharp look Xander drilled into him. "What are you doing? Get down on one knee," they yelled.

Milo frowned, but did as asked. They planted a palm on his shoulder to steady, and picked one foot up.

Oh.

Milo sighed, plans foiled for the moment, and lifted his hands, grimacing as Xander's muddy boot landed in his palms.

He still took the utmost care with his charge despite the less than ideal positioning, and on the count of three, Xander released his shoulder to grab at the sharp edge of the biggest part of the boulder. Their foot pressed into his hand, and in turn, he shoved them higher until their boot left the cradle of his hands entirely. His right arm was dragged above his head as the chain left them connected, but on different platforms.

Before Xander could question him, and wanting to show off a bit himself, he found secure footing, curled his fingers over the jagged edges of the rock face before him, slotting his foot into placement as best he could.

With a prayer on his lips, he scaled the rock, only slipping once or twice, much to his surprise. The rain obscured his vision, and he blinked violently against the downfall.

By the time he made it to the top, Xander looked a *little* more impressed than they had moments ago. He would take it.

When he got to his feet, smile proudly stretched across his lips, he parted his mouth to tell Xander something along the lines of 'suck it' or 'hah, easy' or 'I'm just as impressive as you'.

Instead, a crash of thunder crackled above them, and Milo happened to step on a slick, mossy spot of the boulder at the same moment.

Oh shit.

That was his only thought as he tumbled off the side, down the other side of the boulder.

"Mil—"

Xander's voice was cut off as they had no choice but to tumble with him. He hit the wet ground with a squish, knocking the air out of his lungs yet again.

Blinking against the rain, he barely had time to spy Xander headed for the ground before Milo gasped, and shuffled over. They landed *on* him with a grunt, and Milo coughed out a breath he didn't have room for.

Xander bounced back quickly, having used his internal organs as a landing pad, and they gasped as they sat up, sliding to the ground before turning on him with a grimace.

"God, are you alright?"

Milo nodded, unable to reply because he couldn't catch a fucking breath.

"S'not my name," he finally choked out after Xander had sat him up and leaned him against the boulder that got him in this state in the first place.

It took a split second for the joke to register with Xander, and they rolled their eyes. Was that relief peeking through?

"You must be alright if you're continuing to be a pain in my ass."

When his lungs were in working order, he couldn't help but tease them. "You gotta stop doing that," Milo groused.

"Doing what?" Xander retorted, exasperated.

"Taking my breath away."

Xander's jaw went slack, and Milo's chest cracked wide open at the idea of surprising them yet again.

"I can't believe you," Xander said, and pushed to their feet. "If you're not broken, can we continue?"

"How lucky of me to fall in the direction we were headed anyway."

"Yeah, saved us from having to scale down the rock."

"Anytime. I'll be here all week."

The rest of their trek was less adventurous, nothing but rocks and twigs and a few more fallen trees. Nothing that ended up with him looking like an idiot in front of Xander again.

Finally, once the rain slacked off after what felt like hours, the scent of a fire reached him. "Smell that?" he asked, turning his excitement to share with Xander.

They seemed much less impressed, but altogether relieved. "Someone's burning something."

"We're close, then," Milo murmured.

Their steps hurried, the promise of freedom too good to ignore, too good to waste another minute on. Their conversation dwindled to nothing as they raced through the forest, stepping over roots with ease and knocking branches out of the way, avoiding holes disguised with leaves and twigs.

"They're crafty, these witches," Milo mused aloud.

"I would be too if I lived out in the middle of the fucking forest," Xander drawled.

He saw the first talisman about ten feet ahead, and breathed a sigh of relief, tugging the cuffs to pull Xander to a stop.

"We're here," he said, and tilted his head at the tree. The dangling piece of rock, or metal, or something shimmered softly in the light. Milo would bet money their little home was on the other side of the curve, hidden from any too curious gazes that had made it this far.

"Where's *here*?" Xander questioned, staring out at the forest.

"I think the better question is, who are *you*?" a voice called out to them.

7. A QUEST

Relief settled heavy in Milo's chest as the familiar voice rang through the forest.

"We need your help," Milo called out, taking a step forward.

The talisman glowed momentarily, glaring brighter and brighter. Instinctively, Milo tried to pull Xander behind him, but Xander slapped at his hands until he relented. "Get off me," they hissed.

Abruptly, the glow ended, and the cloaked figure walked away.

Only the sounds of the witch's retreat echoed through the forest, and Milo chanced a look at Xander. "So, do you think we follow, or..."

Xander threw their hands up in exasperation before they followed in the direction of the witch. Their shoulders tensed as they drew near the talisman, and Milo quickened his pace to walk in front of them.

It wasn't a macho thing. Milo was just less likely to die if something magical attacked them.

The chimes dangling from it tinkled in the rain as he passed by, and the glow faded with no consequences. No traps opened up from the forest floor to swallow them whole, no magic binding or whatnot. What *did* witches do these days to keep strangers out?

Maybe Milo would get the chance to ask the witch herself.

Milo walked ahead, though not by much. Xander kept pace with him as they trailed after the cloaked figure.

It was only when they rounded the bend that they stopped in their tracks.

"You're kidding me," Xander breathed.

A grin spread across Milo's face at the awe in their voice, facing the small house.

A picturesque cottage awaited them, complete with colorful foliage and a white picket fence. The porch was lined with wind chimes and talismans and potted plants and even two rocking chairs, though they were empty for the moment.

With an unsure step forward, Xander turned to face him, confusion replacing the awe. "Is it okay to go in?"

The white gate was cracked open, so Milo shrugged, accepting the invitation, and carefully walked over the stepping stone path until they reached the porch.

Would the witch recognize him?

"Hello?" he called out, giving a short and sweet knock on the door.

"It's open," a voice called from inside.

He glanced over his shoulder, only for Xander to make a shooing motion at him. With a roll of his eyes, he twisted the knob, and was hit with the warmth from inside.

However, they were still dripping wet, and one didn't just walk into someones ho—

"Don't worry about the floor, just come in," she said, back still turned to them while she bustled around the kitchen. A roaring fire was flickering in the fireplace, beckoning him with its warmth, and he led Xander across the room to stand before it, soaked clothes be damned.

He glanced over his shoulder at the witch in the small kitchen, red hair long and wild down her back. Her cloak was gone, leaving behind a long floral dress and a muddy pair of boots.

The *drip, drip, drip* of their wet clothes was loud in the house, and they both startled when another voice called out, "Poppy? Who's here?"

They turned as one, and another witch appeared from the hallway, stopping in the mouth of the living room to stare at the two strangers. This witch was blonde, hair in a sharp bob around her face, wearing an oversized sweater and a pair of leggings. A pair of long necklaces jingled slightly as she came to a stop, leaning against the wall at the mouth of the hallway.

"It's Milo. Said he needs my help," Poppy replied with a nod over her shoulder. "Look at them, don't you agree?"

Milo didn't know whether to take offense at that, but hell, if the witch decided to help them, he couldn't exactly mind the pity, could he?

"Mm, yes. I suppose they do look like they've had a rough time of it." Her voice indicated she didn't give a shit about their rough time, and she disappeared down the hallway with an artfully arched brow.

"Tea?" Poppy asked, and turned from the kitchen with a small tray balanced between her hands. The necklace and bracelets she wore clinked against the tray with each step.

Four cups and a small teapot were set before them, porcelain rattling gently as it settled. The fireplace was huge, framed by only two chairs, so Milo sat on the outer hearth, the mountain stone warmed from the heat.

He tugged Xander down with him, ignoring their grunt, and elbowed them in a warning to quit it with the suspicious glares.

Their stare bored into him, and as subtly as possible—that is, not at all—he returned a look that screamed 'chill the fuck out'.

Xander replied with a gaze narrowed and seeming to say 'not on your life', but they relaxed anyway. Even if it seemed forced.

"Tea would be lovely," Milo answered after the awkward delay.

The witch hummed, gaze slipping between the two of them before she took a seat in one of the patchwork chairs angled toward the fire, removing a pillow shaped like a mushroom and tossing it in the remaining chair next to one shaped like a frog.

"While it steeps, you can tell me what the fuck you're doing here."

The calm, gentle tone did not match the words she spoke, and Milo blinked. He parted his lips to respond, only for the blonde witch to return, two towels stacked in her hands. She took a seat in the chair beside Poppy, rotating the pillows to the couch beneath the window, and handed them each a towel.

Milo wrapped it around him like a cloak and scrunched it around his curls, wringing out most of the water.

He couldn't help but notice Xander tossed the towel over their head, and rubbed it into their head haphazardly. His lips twitched.

"This is Iris," Poppy said in that same tone, sharing an equally soft glance with the other witch.

Interesting.

"This is Xander," Milo announced, pulling their attention back to him, instead of gazing at each other with heart eyes.

"We were roleplaying and lost the key." He pointedly avoided Xander's gaze as their head snapped in his direction.

Poppy's lips twitched. "You lost the key?"

Milo nodded reluctantly as Poppy giggled.

"Let me see," Poppy said, waving a hand at them. Milo lifted his left hand out to her, dragging Xander's with it. Poppy hummed as she took his hand, flipping his wrist over and studying the iron. She drifted her touch over it, and his eyes widened at the blue spark that emitted, though he felt nothing from the cuffs themselves.

"Oh, these are *old*," she said, eyes sparking with interest. Her gaze shuttered as she lifted it to Xander. "I don't appreciate being lied to, Milo. What witch do they have locked up doing the hunters' bidding nowadays, hmm? Making cuffs this advanced?"

Xander cocked their head to the side, lowering the towel they'd been drying their hair with and giving nothing away in their expression. "I don't have that information."

Poppy let his wrist go, and Xander crossed their arms with the new freedom, brows furrowed and towel tucked between their arms and their chest.

"It doesn't matter why the cuffs are on, what matters is getting them off. Can you do it?" Milo asked, keeping his tone light.

"I can, yes. Do I want to is the better question," Poppy mused.

Iris's gaze danced between them all as she poured the tea, a smile twitching her lips as she stared at her girlfriend.

These two were disgusting with their smitten little glances and knowing smiles. And they were adorable together, which made it even worse. Milo would put money on that oversized sweater was a hand knitted gift from Poppy.

"What do I get out of helping you?"

"An IOU?" Milo offered.

"Hmm." She stared at them for a long moment, taking the teacup from Iris without breaking her gaze.

Milo accepted the teacup she offered, and then had to lend Xander his cuffed hand so they could reach forward and do the same.

The heat from the fire warmed his back as he waited for Poppy to decide. Lifting the teacup, the warmth soothed over his tongue and down his throat, warming him from the inside out. Out of the corner of his eye, Xander was carefully lifting their teacup one handed, the cuff limiting their range of movement. Without a second thought, Milo scooted over to give them room.

He resisted the urge to smile as they paused before carefully bringing the saucer beneath their tea cup for support. And if their thighs were touching, hip to knee, arms brushing as they sipped tea in the silence of the room, well... That was just a happy accident.

If Xander stiffened even the slightest at the proximity, Milo ignored it, taking an unbothered sip of tea until they did the same.

"Works for me," Poppy said, and Milo's head snapped up to the witch, smile already in place. "Babe, will you go get my spell book from the bedroom?"

Iris placed her tea cup and saucer back on the tray. "Sure, need anything else?" Iris offered as she stood.

Poppy's expression melted into one of a honey sweet adoration as she stared up at her girlfriend. "No, that's all, love."

Once Iris was out of earshot, Poppy leaned forward, voice much less soft. "I will do this under one condition, and one condition only. Do you accept?"

"Do I get to know what the condition is?" Milo asked.

"Do you want the cuffs off or not?" she snapped.

Milo lifted one hand in surrender. "Jeez, fine. Yes, I accept."

"Are you kidding me?" Xander suddenly snapped. "What if she wants your firstborn or something? You're just accepting, just like that?!"

"What do you care? It's *my* firstborn," Milo retorted.

Xander's eyes sharpened into a glare before they shrugged. "I don't. Fine. Whatever."

Poppy's eyes were positively glowing, but she neutralized her expression by the time Iris returned, handing her a large leatherbound book.

"Mmk, I just need..." She flipped through the pages, hemming and hawing before she finally came to a stop. "Oh, yes. This will work. Look! We even have all the ingredients on hand."

Milo tried to lean forward out of pure curiosity, but Poppy snatched up the book and held it to her chest. "Nah, ah. My eyes only, dragon."

Rolling his eyes, Milo settled back into place while she conferred with Iris, holding the page out and pointing to something. Iris seemed to think for a moment before her gaze flittered to them, and then nodded.

Oh, Milo wasn't so sure about this.

What was Poppy up to now?

He narrowed his gaze. The last time he'd seen her, she'd been hanging from the bicep of an orc like she was a pull-up bar, singing at the top of her lungs in Patty's tavern.

What had happened there?

He shared an unsure glance with Xander, who glared right back at him as if to say *I told you so*.

They jumped, tea cups clattering as Poppy slammed the book shut with a smack. "Alright! Let's get this shindig started."

The *shindig* turned out to be a private little kitchen

cooking lesson between the two witches while they brewed up some kind of concoction. Xander and Milo were banished to finish drying by the fire.

Unfortunately, it meant Milo and Xander had a front row seat to their flirting, visible through the framed window-like cut outs of the wall between.

The witches moved around the kitchen together as if they were two halves of the same whole, always aware of the other's presence and dancing around in harmony. It *had* to be some kind of foreplay for them, the way they kept sliding past one another with their hands chastely placed upon the other's hip, back, or upper arm.

Milo shared an exasperated look with Xander, only to find that Xander wasn't even paying attention to him. They were watching the witches giggle and laugh with one another, soft exchanges shared in the privacy of the kitchen while the fire crackled behind them.

"They're cute," Milo said softly.

It startled Xander out of their reverie, and they shot him a confused look. "Yeah. I guess."

After that, they pointedly stared into their tea, all while Milo racked his brain trying to decipher that look.

Almost confusion, but *not*. Almost annoyance, but *not*. Almost jealousy? But also *not*.

Eventually, their gaze returned to the witches at another outburst of giggling, and Milo finally got it.

Longing.

Milo understood *that*. Wanting someone who just *clicked* with you. Effortlessly. Without the awkwardness of getting to know one another, without the doubt or confusion or games. As a hunter, did Xander have friends? What did they do, sit around and talk about the dragons they'd bagged, the hoards they'd scored over drinks?

Hunters were notoriously cruel, unwelcome in *most*

places now that Others were integrating with the rest of the world. Milo had only met another hunter once in his life.

A cruel, old bastard decades ago. Milo had barely escaped with his life, and could still recall the snarl on that man's face as they'd fought. The disgust twisted on his lips, the greed shining from his eyes as he asked Milo about his hoard.

Milo could *not* reconcile his knowledge of hunters with the person sitting beside him, gazing at the flirting witches with something akin to awe.

But Xander was a fortress, giving nothing away, especially when directly asked. Maybe this would remain a mystery.

He frowned. Xander *was* a hunter. And hunters were after one thing: Treasure.

And Milo wasn't going to give up his treasure. Or his scales.

So what happened once the cuffs were off? Milo wasn't giving his hoard up, and Xander didn't seem like one for failure, so… what next?

Just as he leaned over to offer Xander the same question, Poppy clapped her hands and called out to them. "It's ready. Let's go!"

Xander stood first, eagerly taking a step forward, having finished their tea ages ago. Milo, however, swallowed his questions and stood a bit slower, but followed after them dutifully.

Iris stayed in the kitchen, waving after them with a smirk. The kitchen door led out into the back yard, where a full on garden was in bloom, greenery thriving in neat little rows. The stepping stones weaved them down the middle to a fire pit, where chopped logs were arranged in a circle for guests to sit on.

But they didn't stop there either. They continued a little further, past a manicured clover lawn to where their property supposedly ended. He could tell because it went from flourishing clover to the muddy dirt of the forest floor.

"You stand here," she said to Milo, and then tugged Xander by the arm directly across from him.

"Stretch the chain out, please."

Milo and Xander stood about two feet apart, the chain stretched out between their wrists, cuffs dark and aggressive against their skin.

"Do we need to do anything?" Milo asked.

"Yep, just sip this for me," Poppy said, lifting out two shot glasses. One had a 3-D flamingo hanging off the side.

"Really?" Xander drawled. "Why do we have to drink something? You're unlocking the *cuffs*."

"And *who* are the cuffs attached to, dear?" she asked, voice sharper than the words themselves.

Milo tilted his shot glass against his lips, the liquid thick like medicine and sliding down no more pleasantly. He grimaced, but urged Xander to do the same.

Poppy was not a witch to mess with, and the longer they were in her presence, the more of a chance Xander had of pissing her off.

That was not what Milo wanted out of this whole mess.

Hell, what did he want out of this?

Xander stared down at the liquid in their glass, but ultimately tipped it against their lips and swallowed it down just like Milo had.

They coughed, wincing at the taste.

"Don't insult my cooking," Poppy scoffed, and took the glasses back with a slight smile. "Now I've just gotta chant a few words, and the cuffs should fall away. Stay still."

Milo wondered if there was a school all witches went to in order to learn whatever language they spoke in. Did they have to learn the cadence as well? Was it like a song and each spell had its own beat?

To his ears, it sounded like any other boring old chant, but the power in her words was undeniable.

He caught Xander's gaze as she chanted over them, lifting her hands over the chain.

A grimace stained their features, and he wondered if it was the aftertaste of the potion or the idea of magic in general.

As a hunter, they must have known dragons existed longer than the rest of the human race, and with that, other supernatural creatures too. What was with the disdain when it came to witches? Or magic?

Fuck, he had so many questions for them. They grew in multitudes every minute he spent with them.

And they seemed less than open to answering them, but damned if that'd stop him.

His attention was dragged back to the cuff as it grew heated against his skin. The symbols etched into the metal glowed bright, casting shadows around them. He winced at the light, averting his gaze to the side. Along the way, he caught Xander's wide eyed stare *into* the glow.

He couldn't tell if they were alarmed or afraid or just frozen in a state of awe, and before he could do *anything*, the cuffs rattled and then fell away, landing on the forest floor with a clank.

"That was… so. Fucking. Cool," Xander breathed.

Milo's lips twitched as humor tickled his chest. Of *course* they weren't afraid. They were… Xander!

"Excellent," Poppy said, pride filling her voice. "Now. You *are* a treasure hunter, yes?" the witch asked, lowering her voice, and turning to lead them back to the fire pit.

Xander's gaze darted to Milo's as they followed her. He would almost say for reassurance, but Xander would never search *him* out for something like that.

"Yes," they answered finally.

Poppy spun around as they reached the firepit, expression lighting up. "Good. You," she pointed to Milo. "Sit."

Milo sat on one of the overturned logs.

"And you," she said, turning her gaze to Xander, who stared at the witch with unhindered suspicion. "Go stand over there."

Xander narrowed their gaze, but this time, when they sought out Milo, he offered a nod. The cuffs were off, so Xander should be taking every chance they could get to get away from—

"Fuck!" he gasped, lurching to his feet at the tightening in his chest. Like someone had cranked all his ribs too tight, squeezing and shifting and crushing his vital organs.

The witch cackled, grabbed his hand, and tugged him toward Xander.

Their eyes were wide, and they clutched at their own chest, but the pain was lessening with each step. By the time they were only a few feet apart, the pain was gone completely, only the memory of it a sharp reminder.

Xander glanced down at their hands, sliding across their flat chest in swift, staccato movements as if they expected blood to drip from their palms.

"What the *hell?*" they barked sharply, and *oh.* That tone did something to Milo that he wasn't going to look too closely at.

The witch seemed unaffected by whatever spell Xander was weaving over him, and shrugged. "I need a favor. This ensures your cooperation."

The cuffs were gone, but they were still as linked as ever. Their gazes clashed, and in Xander's, a fire raged.

"What's the favor?" Milo asked, sliding between the witch and Xander, lest the latter attack their only chance at true separation.

Poppy's gaze trailed back to the house, toward Iris, visible through the kitchen window, the lines around her eyes softening.

Ah.

"I need a ring," she finally said, lifting her attention to them once again. "And you're going to get it for me."

8. FLIGHT FOR TWO

Xander was fuming.

They smacked branches out of their way, kicked rocks only to hear them crash through the foliage, and muttered curses all the way through the forest.

It wasn't until they were almost to the car that a hand curled around their wrist and pulled them to a stop.

"I'm only stopping you now because I don't want you to hurt the car," Milo said, and Xander could *hear* his stupid smile in the words.

Xander huffed a breath, refusing to face the goddamned dragon.

"An engagement ring? Really?" Xander bit out.

"From her ex. Yep."

"You've gotta be fucking kidding me."

"No jokes here, unfortunately."

Milo was too calm about this, and that pissed them off all over again.

"I don't suppose you've already concocted a plan to get this ring back?" they snapped, finally whirling on Milo and making him drop the soothing rhythm he'd begun massaging over their pulse point.

He lifted his hands in surrender. "Of the two of us, I was

kinda hoping you would have a plan. Since you're a treasure hunter and all."

Xander pointedly ignored the twitch to his lips. "Yes, I'm a fucking treasure hunter," they bit out quickly. "Doesn't mean I know how to rob some... some fucking—"

"An orc. You can say it."

"Why would Poppy even need *that* ring? It's—you said we could trust her!" Xander snapped.

Milo held his hands out, brows muddling in concern. "And we could! She got the cuffs off, didn't she!"

Xander grit their teeth in his direction. Ohhh, they could *throttle* this dragon. "At what cost? We're still bound together! It makes no difference!"

"Aw, come on," Milo lifted a hand to his chest. "I'm not so bad, am I? So eager to get away?"

Annoyance flared bright and hot in their chest, and they took a step forward. Milo danced back—*but not too far*, they noted—with a contrite expression. "Okay, okay! Look, it won't be that hard, right? She said the orc wears it on a neck-lace. Just a sleight of hand trick, that's all."

"What if the orc isn't in the place Poppy said?"

"Well, that's where we can start. It's not too terribly far from here."

Xander swallowed their next words as a vibration buzzed in their pocket. With a curse, they dug their cell phone out and sighed at the display. "*Don't* say anything," they warned sharply.

Turning their back on the dragon, they paced a few steps away, just far enough for their chest to tighten, before they came to a stop and answered the call.

"Xander," they answered.

"It's been seventy-two hours," was their greeting. No hello, hey, glad you aren't dead. "Progress report?"

"I've run into some... complications. But I'm handling it, it's just taking longer than expected."

The silence on the line spoke volumes. "Do I need to send in backup?"

They let their gaze flutter shut out of mortification. "No, sir. I'm handling it, like always. Do I ever disappoint?"

"I'll refrain from repeating what you already know," he said, tone dripping with disapproval.

It was a tone Xander knew intimately.

"Yes, sir," they said, the correct response ingrained in them from years and years of listening to him berate the hunters.

"You know what's at stake. How important each mission is. Keep that in mind. And *don't* hesitate to call in if you've become compromised."

Xander winced. "Of course."

What did one consider compromised? Where was the line?

Xander suspected they'd passed it years ago.

"You know how to reach us."

He hung up without another word and Xander sighed, gripping the phone tight in their hand.

It buzzed another time, and they lowered it to view the screen. A text from Caleb, one of the hunters, awaited them.

I heard that. He's in a mood today. Be safe.

Xander sighed, lips twitching into a small smile deite the situation.

Always.

The response was immediate, before Xander could even lower the device.

Liar. I know you, that's why I said be safe.

They sent an eye-roll emoji—very professional—before tucking the phone in their pocket. *Fuck.*

"Everything alright?" Milo asked, voice a lot closer than he should be.

Xander whirled around, not even having recognized the tightness in their chest ease with his proximity. "Yes. Yeah. Everything's fine."

"Hmm. Something tells me you just lied," Milo mused. "I thought we were pals?"

The stupid fake sad frown on his lips was just itching to be slapped off his handsome face.

Xander glared. "Fine. When this started I was given seventy-two hours. Guess how long it's been?"

Milo's eyes widened, and Xander cheered just a little at the fresh panic in his gaze. "What does that mean?"

"It means I've been given a warning to hurry the fuck up. For now... we need to get this over with if you don't want the fucking Hunters of Obscure Artifacts knocking at your door."

"Well, what are we waiting on?" Milo asked, and turned away from Xander to head to the car.

"That's what I've been *saying*," Xander bit out, grumbling beneath their breath.

"I heard that," Milo sang.

Rolling their eyes, Xander followed behind Milo and climbed in the car from their own door.

"I'll never take for granted having my hands to myself again," Milo vowed as the door slammed shut behind them.

"You're telling me," Xander grumbled, imagining the pile of clothes still on Milo's bathroom floor. After buckling their seatbelt, they leaned back against the seat and shut their eyes. "I can't wait to put on something besides this useless poncho."

"Aw, come on," Milo teased. "It hasn't grown on you yet?"

They rolled their head on the seat to glare at the dragon

as he started the car with a rumble and turned it around. "No."

"You wound me," he said, voice still light.

"So what's the plan?" Xander asked, closing their eyes again as the car hugged curve after curve.

"Orcs love dragons, you know. We're like puppies for them. Not to say they don't love *actual* puppies, but we're less… breakable than puppies."

"Say puppies one more time," Xander warned, trying not to find this dragon impossibly endearing. A harder task than it sounded, and growing more difficult by the hour. Even as pissed as they were at the witches, the cuffs *were* off.

"Well… I say we find the orc at this bar, right? I'll distract them by going dragon, and you can swipe the necklace from her."

"Oh, so I'm the one with the important job while you play bait?" Xander responded.

It wasn't until the silence in the car grew too loud that they realized they'd just *teased* Milo.

Oh no.

You're a fucking hunter, man. Act like it.

"Just like a dragon to take the easy way out," they added casually.

"There it is," Milo said.

How did he *do* that? Inject his smile into every word he spoke, in spite of Xander being a dick.

Even as infuriating as it was, their chest ached with fondness. Which was stupid. It hadn't even *been* seventy-two hours, and this dragon had disarmed Xander with nothing but his stupid smile and his trinkets and his… just *him.*

Maybe Xander was already compromised. Maybe they *should* let Arthur call in backup.

No, calling in the other hunters was signing Milo's death

warrant. And as much as Xander liked to pretend otherwise, they did have a heart beating in their chest.

They still had time, though it was dwindling quicker than they could control. They could still turn this around; there was still a chance. All they had to do was steal a ring and return it to the witches.

And along the way, Xander would convince Milo to give them his treasure hoard.

They had to.

But for now, they just needed to get this damned ring back.

"I dunno, I mean at least we can get dressed now, yeah? The bond isn't *that* bad," Milo said from the other side of the bathroom door.

Xander rolled their eyes, turned their face up to the water, trying unsuccessfully to ignore the man who wouldn't let them shower in peace. "Try telling me that when you *don't* have to be present during my showers."

"At least you have both hands this time."

A pause.

"Can I come in? My chest fucking hurts!"

The pain in their chest was only minimal, at best. "You're just a baby!" Xander called out.

Xander picked out a different scent from Milo's wild collection from the inset shelf in the shower. It had flowers on the packaging, but the smell wasn't cloying, didn't suffocate them like the usual stuff did. They missed the comfort of their usual sea salt and lemongrass, but Milo's flowers would have to do.

"That's toxic! I'm coming in."

"Don't you d—" But it was too late. The door shut softly behind the dragon, and Xander huffed a sigh as they lathered up a loofah and began scrubbing the rain and dirt from their skin.

The pain in their chest eased, and they risked a peek through the curtain to find Milo had hopped up onto the counter, leaning back against the mirror with his eyes closed. "See? Doesn't that feel better?"

Ignoring him, Xander tried not to overthink the plan they'd come up with in the car. It was created on shaky enough foundation, it probably couldn't withstand all the ways Xander could poke and prod until it fell apart.

So they finished their shower quickly, dried off, and stepped out all while Milo kept his eyes closed. They made sure the towel was in place around their hips before clearing their throat.

It didn't much matter if Milo saw their chest scars at this point. In fact, Xander *wanted* him to see.

They tried not to dwell too much on *why*.

"Your turn."

Milo opened one eye to peek before sliding off the counter. "Brought you some more clothes. They should fit. Too small for me, but I really like the pattern on the shirt so I never threw it out."

"Thanks," Xander offered as Milo scooted past them.

Wow, that was almost a normal interacti—

"No peeking at my jewels, now," Milo drawled.

Xander's eye twitched, but damn it all if their lips didn't twitch too, a smile trying to carve itself onto their face.

"Wouldn't dream of it," they finally responded, probably after far too long of a pause to be reasonable.

They ignored Milo humming as they dried and dressed. The pattern on the shirt was wild, loud in ways Xander had only seen on television, or on other people walking down the street.

But damn was it soft and silky, and the stiff collar made it lay across their chest like it was fucking made for their frame. Was this shit tailored?

It was a little—okay, a lot—weird to be wearing the dragon's clothes, but...

But...

It looked nice, alright? Xander felt comfortable, making the confidence they felt settle on their shoulders better.

Xander left the top two buttons undone, the gap in the shirt showing off the expanse of their torso, the harness framing their pecs and the scars circling the underside of their areola if one squinted.

They felt fucking *good* in front of the mirror. The pants didn't fit as snugly as they could have, but they weren't falling down their hips, and that's all they could ask for.

Milo's shower cut off after they'd been dressed, and ohh was it a power trip to watch Milo falter as he pulled the shower curtain back. A towel was already wrapped around his waist.

He lifted one foot out of the tub when his gaze locked and landed on Xander. Lowering his foot without looking was a mistake, as he missed the rug, stepped on the slick floor, and slipped.

"Milo!" Xander called out, hands darting forward as if to catch him.

Milo's left foot, the one that lost control on its way to the floor, slid out and knocked into Xander's feet when they rushed to help. The collision shoved their feet out from beneath them, and they landed with an *oof* on top of Milo.

On *top* of Milo.

The situation dawned on them slowly, and Xander froze, face millimeters from a very naked, very muscled chest.

Their legs were all tangled up, hips crushed together. Xander was afraid to see if the towel was still in place.

Milo inhaled sharply, and suddenly paused, pulled his head back until he met Xander's gaze. "Hey, you used my favorite body wash," he said, voice soft and low and far, far too velvety.

They were too close for Xander's comfort, but Milo was all wet and slippery and smelled *really* nice. Actually, he smelled the same as Xander. Dammit, the dragon was right.

"It's a nice scent," Xander breathed, eyes wide at their proximity, and the apparent lack of disgust.

No. Right then, disgust was the last thing on their mind.

A buzzing from the vanity shattered the moment and Xander cursed, scrambling to get off the floor. They only slipped once, barely holding onto their dignity by the time they swiped their phone off the counter.

It was Caleb. Again. It'd been what? A few hours?

"What?" Xander hissed in greeting.

The disapproval was heavy in his pause before he spoke. "There's been a development you should know about."

"What is it?"

"We think we got false intel about one of the in progress missions."

Xander paused. "What? Why?"

"There were two dragons on the premises, not just one. An… unexpected complication. I can't share too many details, but keep an eye open. If *you* need backup, call. I'm serious, Xander. No matter what Arthur says, I'll be there if you need it."

Did the hunter make it out alive? What happened?

Xander had to choke on their questions, because they were more focused on his last line. What did he mean, no matter what Arthur says? Caleb had been their backup on more than one occasion, why would Arthur suddenly interfere with that?

Instead, they huffed out a sigh. "You're usually the one that needs *my* help, remember? Have I ever failed before?" Xander asked quietly.

"There's a first time for everything," Caleb drawled.

Oh, *that* irked them. "I've never failed to bring back a hoard before and you know it. Now leave me alone until my mission is complete. At this point, *you're* the one in danger of fucking it up."

They could practically hear his eye roll. "Fine. See you when your mission is complete."

Xander hung up without responding, their chest tight and adrenaline running high.

The annoyance of the call helped them forget what happened in the bathroom with Milo... right up until Milo cleared his throat.

Xander spun around, found Milo in the doorway of the bathroom with a grimace on his face. "That sounded pleasant."

It's a nice scent?!

Jesus, Xander, way to be a fucking lame ass.

Not that it mattered. Because Xander wasn't interested in Milo. Not at all. Actually, the lamer the better.

They could just appreciate his fancy clothes and bath products. And the coffee. And the nice car. Of course. Yeah, that was all.

"You know, the word pleasant rarely comes to mind when talking to him."

"He sounds like a *lovely* guy," Milo said, sarcasm dripping from the words.

Xander checked the time on their phone. "How far away is the bar? Are you ready?"

Milo most certainly looked it, in floral patterned pants

and a dark button up that snugged his pecs in a distracting way.

Distracting for someone else, of course. Because Xander wasn't interested.

"Do I look ready?" Milo asked, holding his hands out at his side, expectant expression on his face.

"Riiight," they drawled, under no obligation to answer that. "Let's go."

"I assume you're going to make me drive again?" Milo asked, and grabbed two jackets from the coat rack, handing one off to Xander. It was a little too large in the shoulders, but fuck it. The leather matched their boots.

"I would rather not fly. Like, what if I fell off?" they asked.

It wasn't like Dragon Riding was in the *other* category of their resume.

However, Milo looked downright affronted at their words. "As if I'd let you fall off. Come on, let me fly!"

Xander suddenly understood why orcs often referred to dragons as puppies. Milo was the fucking epitome of the word, practically bouncing on his toes.

"Fine, fine!" Xander snapped, trying not to let their smile show. "You can—"

"Yes! Let's go." Milo rushed to pull open the door, the cooler summer evening air rushing in. As he bounded to the middle of the yard, Xander watched from the porch rail.

Crossing their arms, they leaned against one of the posts on the porch and tried to keep the fizziness in their chest contained. It was an annoying fluttery, light feeling, and Xander hated it just because they didn't know what it was.

Their thoughts derailed as Milo finally changed.

It happened so fast. If Xander had blinked, they would've missed it. The dragon exploded out of Milo, but not in a violent way. Fuck, they couldn't even describe it. A wave of scales washed over him and then a dragon was on Milo's lawn in place of the man himself.

"Holy shit," they blurted, and jumped over the railing to rush out to him.

The dragon sat there, like out of every fantasy novel. His brown eyes were still Milo, even his mannerisms. He settled down to the ground like a puppy about to play, head low and yeah, Xander totally got it now.

Dragons were *cute.*

Funny that, Xander never having actually seen a dragon. The way they usually operated, the dragons never got a chance to shift. They'd never had the opportunity, until now.

"You're really fuckin' pretty," Xander told him as they approached.

Milo's eyes were locked on them as they approached, and Xander lifted a hand. They waited until Milo gave them a little nod before placing their hand on his arm.

He was fucking huge, too. Even with his snout lowered to the ground, they were *still* eye level.

Milo's eyes darted to the side, and he tilted his head back.

"Okay, okay," Xander agreed, walking a few paces back and unsure of how to proceed. "I've never exactly ridden a dragon before, so—oh!"

Milo held a clawed hand behind them at the same time he shoved his neck closer, and Xander jumped at the last second, the hand guiding them into position over the back of Milo's neck.

"A little warning would be n—holy fucking shit!"

Their shout was lost in the wind as Milo flapped his wings, wind rushing around them.

Xander's hands grappled over shiny, smooth scales, until they finally found somewhere they could hold onto. They squeezed their thighs around his broad neck, heart thundering in their head louder than the rushing noise of the wind.

Heights had never been their favorite, but they couldn't help but look over the side, watching the house grow smaller and smaller and then disappearing from view altogether.

They had no clue how fast they were going, but their hair whipped around their face and the warm night air made their clothes flap. If they weren't so tense, so worried about falling to their death, they might have zipped the borrowed leather jacket up.

They caressed the smooth scales under their palms, shiny and copper if you glanced from one direction, and dark as night from any other angle.

Leave it to Milo to be gorgeous in both human and dragon form.

Not that... not that Xander was attracted to him, of course.

Milo was taking them somewhere far, they finally realized after about a half hour. The wind was growing colder, and eventually they had to risk death to zip their jacket up.

Xander didn't know how Milo did it. Sometimes his wings would shift steadily behind their back, and other times they would feel the way he stiffened, let the air currents carry him to where they needed to go.

To an *orc* bar.

When they finally arrived, a much longer flight than Xander had anticipated, they already had a few sets of eyes their way.

Milo landed them gently, and Xander slid off, thighs a little shaky from holding them so tense for so long. Not that they'd ever admit it.

The shift was just as quick as it had been the first time, and the dragon melted down to Milo's familiar form. His grin was quick and sharp and just pure happiness. "That was fucking awesome. You're a great passenger."

"Thanks? It was a pretty smooth flight."

"Did you get cold?" he asked with a wink, nodding down to the borrowed jacket and the full zip.

"Yes! I had to risk my life to zip this up, I'll have you know. I could've slipped right off."

Milo rolled his eyes, but waited for them to adjust their shirt again—had to get the gaping right—before he held out his arm.

Xander narrowed their eyes, but, since it was part of their cover, wrapped their arm in his. Side by side, they made their way into the bar.

A few orcs said hello without so many words. More of a nod, or a fistbump for Milo as the doorman let them pass.

"*Told you, they love dragons,*" Milo leaned close and bragged.

Yeah, yeah.

Xander never really cared much for bars, whether in human run cities or the small communities *Others* had created for themselves after the Big Reveal.

"So what's the plan?" they asked, as Milo led them to a table.

"Well, we need to wait a little. It's still early, they're not drunk yet."

Milo had a point, and Xander was a little annoyed they hadn't considered it.

Besides their early training days, Xander hadn't ever worked alongside anyone else, besides bailing Caleb out of trouble every now and then.

The only person you could trust was yourself and all that.

It would be funny, if only it hadn't been proven true over and over again.

Besides. What Xander did?

Another hunter would never sanction it.

That's why Xander worked alone. Why Xander would *always* work alone.

"We need to fit in, so I'll go grab us drinks. Any requests?" Milo pulled them from their thoughts with a harmless grin.

"Just get me whatever," Xander replied.

They watched as Milo crossed the bar, greeting a few orcs and accepting the back pats and—

Xander snorted as one of them ruffled his hair, watched from afar as Milo grinned to his face and then frowned as soon as he turned away, fluffing his curls back into some semblance of order.

The fizziness, like a shaken soda, returned, and Xander wondered if maybe they should get checked out by the physician when this was all over.

He returned moments later with their drinks, and Xander wrapped a hand around the chilled glass and leaned forward.

"How is this gonna work? What if she doesn't have the ring anymore? Got rid of it along with memories of a bad ex?"

Milo arched a brow and sipped his drink. "Who says Poppy was the bad ex, huh?"

"Oh, sorry. Pardon me for assuming the witch who wants us to steal a gift back was the bad guy in this scenario."

"She never gave the ring to Sharn. Sharn stole it from her because she knew it was a family heirloom. Were you not listening to the story at all?"

Xander grumbled and leaned back, finally taking a sip of their drink.

It burned, like all whiskey did, but the burn was smooth and vanilla, cherry, and smoke.

"Oo this is nice," Xander remarked, bringing the glass back down and appreciating the amber liquid.

If Milo's gaze was warm and yummy just like the bourbon, Xander refused to notice. Refused.

Xander hummed and returned to picking apart their shoddy plan. "What if she doesn't show? It's Monday."

"Exactly. It's a Monday. Where would *you* go after a shitty day at work?"

"The…"

Xander squinted. "Shooting range?"

"Bar," Milo said at the same time, and then shook his head. "Now you're just being difficult," Milo chastised.

"Right, of course," Xander agreed, as if they'd known all along what the right answer was. As if they hadn't unbuttoned this shirt on purpose, their own plan in mind in case Milo's failed.

Milo was a little too easy to play with, and if he looked at their chest *one* more time—

His gaze dipped to the split V of the shirt, the harness underneath, and Xander *denied* the twitch on their lips.

Milo clearly found them attractive, and the knowledge was… alright, they'd admit it.

Heady. Delicious, in a guilty pleasure kind of way.

"So, what's our escape route?" Xander asked.

Milo cocked his head to the side. "Uh… Get the ring and run?"

Xander paused, slowly lifting their gaze from the drink to stare at Milo. "We're in a bar full of orcs."

"Yes."

"A bar full. As in multiple," they clarified, as if Milo had somehow missed the multiple green men and women around them.

"Yep."

"And you just want to… run?"

Was this guy crazy? Or just stupid?

"What happens if she figures it out? If she gets pissed and the whole bar turns against us?"

"Just don't get caught," Milo drawled, chancing a quick look at them in the low lighting. "Something tells me you're good at that."

"Yeah, yeah," Xander groaned, and leaned back in their seat. "Treasure hunter, we all know."

"You *can* get the necklace off her, yes? During the distraction?"

"Do I *look* like an amateur?" Xander cut back.

9. A HEIST

Xander looked like a lot of things in that low cut, artfully opened shirt, leather flashing beneath in a tantalizing harness. An amateur was not the first thing that came to mind.

"Hmm," Milo pretended to think on it. "No, I guess you're not an amateur."

"You guess?" Xander practically snarled, cheeks heating with indignation. "You little…"

Milo winked at them, just to get their blood pressure up.

With a huff, they sipped their whiskey again and cast a furtive glance around the room. Probably clocking the exits and internalizing an escape route, or whatever hunters were trained to do.

"So. This is an orc community," Xander noted.

Milo tilted his head. "Yeah?"

"Why don't dragons have a community? You're all spread out."

"Well, dragons are territorial. We like our space. And before now… we'd been in hiding too. It'd paint a pretty target on our backs if suddenly humans were sighting flocks of winged creatures."

Xander hummed, seeming less impressed with the information.

"You know we're from Hell, right?" Milo asked.

That got Xander's eyes to widen. "What?" they questioned.

Milo nodded. "Yep. Lucifer took a step back from being such an asshole, and most of us left."

"Did he not care?"

"We're not really sure what happened. To be honest, even if he did try to recall us back to Hell, I don't even know where to begin to find us all."

"Riiiiight," Xander dragged out the vowel until Milo's lips twitched.

"I'll let you process."

Xander nodded, gaze boring into Milo with their brow furrowed.

Don't look at their chest—too late. Fuck.

Clearing their throat, Xander gave him a pointed glare. Right. Milo should try to be less obvious.

"I, uh… closed my bakery," he said to fill the now awkward silence, thanks to his rogue eyeballs glancing where they didn't belong. "Y'know, while we're doing this," he said, motioning between them.

As Xander arched a brow, warmth rushed to Milo at the implication. "Not *this*," he said, hand waving back and forth again. "I mean the mission. The quest. Getting the ring b—"

"I get it," Xander drawled.

Milo sighed and sipped his bourbon in aggravated silence. Averting his gaze, he let it wander around the room, only to pause as the orcs in front of their table began to laugh, swaying back and forth and allowing a gap between their bodies.

Through that gap, he spied a familiar orc woman, dark

hair braided over one shoulder and laughing at something another man said.

"Don't be so obvious," Xander snapped, literally, their fingers clicking in front of his face. "You're just now noticing her?"

Milo blinked back at Xander and waved their hand away. "I couldn't see her until now," he retorted.

Xander rolled their eyes, and Milo wondered if he was imagining the fondness that twitched their lips.

"Well, since you can clearly see her *so* well," Milo drawled, "maybe you could tell me if she's actually wearing the ring we're here to retrieve?"

Xander nodded. "Yep. On a leather cord around her neck, just like the witch said."

Excitement zipped up Milo's spine. "Awesome. So now we just—"

Xander suddenly tipped their glass back, and Milo watched the bourbon slip down their throat.

Then they stood, and Milo tore himself from his less than holy thoughts. "Wait, where are you going—"

"It's time for plan B. Sit back and watch."

Xander disappeared into the throng of people before Milo could protest. To keep up appearances, he lifted the bourbon to his lips and took a drink.

It was good, but not as good as Patty's brew. He'd have to tell her.

Ow, ow, ow.

His chest tightened, squeezed, ribs crunching and grinding in ways they weren't supposed to as the invisible bond between him and Xander was stretched thin.

It eased finally, but there was no sign of Xander still. Granted, the bar's large patrons obscured most of the surroundings.

Orcs were huge, even the shortest ones scaling above Milo and Xander both.

To some people, it might be intimidating.

Those people were *not* Xander, as it turns out.

Moments later, when a pair of orcs stood from their table to leave, they revealed Xander, and Milo almost spit the bourbon out all over the table.

He swallowed, the drink going down like a handful of tacks, and trained his wide eyes on Xander's form.

They were leaned up against the orc's table, positioned in such a way that their shirt gaped open, showing off their leather harness. Sharn, however, was enraptured, as if Xander was just the snack she was looking for.

Her grin was wide, and Sharn raised her hand to the bartender, who glanced her way with a nod before getting busy making whatever concoctions she clearly ordered often.

Oh no. Sharn was a regular. And popular, as could be determined by the huge crowd at her table.

And there Xander was, right in the center of it all, spinning a story, arms and gloved hands moving for dramatic effect.

The table burst out in loud, raucous laughter, heads tilted back, hands smacking the table and knees alike.

A smile curled Xander's lips in a way that stirred heat in Milo's gut.

And he wasn't the only one.

Sharn motioned them closer, and Xander sidled right up to her side before she scooped Xander up and planted them on her lap.

Oh… Milo *hated* this.

The *tiniest* bit of annoyance flashed across Xander's expression—giving him hope that maybe Xander hated it too —but they buried it as quickly as it'd unearthed itself. They turned a smitten expression up to the orc, mouthing something else Milo couldn't make out, and leaned their head back in a laugh.

So Xander was a naturally talented flirt.

That was fine. Totally fine.

In fact, it was so *fine* that Milo leaned back in his chair and sipped his bourbon. Xander could clearly handle this situation. Without him.

Milo kept his expression perfectly neutral as the orcs' laughter grew more obnoxious.

If Xander was so good at flirting, why hadn't they just continued to flirt with Milo instead of cuffing them together? They didn't seem the type to panic. So *why* move too early?

He narrowed his gaze.

Was *that* part of their game? Make Milo think they were in danger with this supervisor, some poor schmuck who couldn't catch a break?

Because...because it was *totally* working. Fuck. Was he really that easy?

Milo *already* had a soft spot for this stupid hunter.

And yes, fine. It *was* jealousy curling up behind his ribs and twisting mercilessly.

Alright. Milo needed to put an end to this sooner rather than later. He needed to get this hunter out of his fucking hair so he could go back to enjoying his fancy shit alone, without worrying about some hunter taking off with it.

He downed the rest of his bourbon just like Xander had, and stood from his table. The chair scraped back with an obnoxious screech, drawing the attention of a few orcs nearby.

Good. The bigger the audience, the better.

He put a little sway in his steps and approached the table. The orcs were hanging onto every word spun from Xander's lips, especially Sharn, eyes glowing bright with a sizable… crush.

Like recognized like, and all that.

Milo hummed. "I don't remember agreeing to this part of our date," he slurred, interrupting Xander's story.

They froze, their arm curled around the back of the orc's neck, before slowly turning to him with a confused glare. "What?"

"I mean, I *fly* you here on my own back, and now you're sitting in an orc's lap? What the hell, Sunshine?"

Xander's eye twitched at the pet name, and Milo's chest exploded into fizzy excitement.

"I thought we agreed to try things as friends first. You're being a shitty wingman," they growled.

"*Wing*man? Is this cause I'm a dragon? I thought that didn't bother you!" he whined.

"You know damned well it doesn't," Xander shot back. "We agreed this was an open relationship."

Milo groaned. "Oh please! You know how easy I cave to whatever you want when you have me tied up like you did last night!"

"Oh shit, this is getting good," Sharn said, a laugh in her words as Xander's arm lowered from her neck.

Xander smiled tightly at him and turned back to the orc. "I'm so sorry about this, really. He's just so…" They squeezed their hands as if choking someone out. "Frustrating."

The orc giggled. Yes, *giggled*, and waved Xander off. "Go have a chat with your… wingman. I'll be here."

Xander brushed a lock of her dark hair behind her ear, making the orc *blush* before Xander slid off her lap.

They stared up at Milo with a glare before fisting the front of his shirt and dragging him toward the front door, ignoring the catcalls and whistles that followed them.

The door slammed behind them with a clang, and Xander turned on him. "*What* was that?"

"Did you get it?" he asked.

Xander lifted the leather cord and ring from their pocket with a grimace. "Of course I did. You doubted me?"

"Not for a second," Milo said, annoyed to find that it was the absolute truth. "You adjusted quickly."

"I've had lots of practice," they drawled, walking away from the bar, toward the parking lot. "Ready to get out of here?"

In answer, Milo followed them through the lot, past a few rows of SUVs. Not quite your average sedan sitting in this lot.

There was a lightness to Xander's steps that Milo hadn't seen before. "You're a pretty good actor yourself, given the circumstances."

The circumstances at hand reminded Milo that he wasn't supposed to give into this act anymore.

It took them a moment to realize Milo wasn't following them anymore, and Milo was waiting when they finally turned toward him.

"What is it—oh. You're mad," Xander guessed, a lilt of disbelief to their tone.

"Yes, I'm mad," Milo snapped. "So many things could've gone wrong with your plan—"

"Oh, as if your plan was any better?"

"—what if you weren't their type? Huh? And she turned you down?"

Xander scoffed. "Please. I'm everyone's type."

Milo's brows scrunched together, he could *feel* it, and tried to wipe the frown off his face, to arrange it into something more neutral.

"I'm sorry, do you disagree?" Xander drawled.

Of course not, Milo wanted to say, but somehow that felt like giving away more than he was ready for.

You're *my* type, and that's all that matters.

But he kept that thought to himself.

"I just can't help but think—"

He was interrupted by the slam and clang of the bar door, and a shout. "There they are! Get them!" the brunette orc yelled, fury in her words as she charged in their direction.

"Oh, shit," Milo hissed. He didn't even bother trying to pull Xander behind him this time.

They were already twirling a knife.

One of the larger orcs charged for Milo, and he ducked a head-sized fist, backing away with his hands held in front of him. "Okay, listen. We can talk about *this*—"

He dodged again, putting a car between them for safety.

The orc slammed his fist into an open palm, cracking his knuckles with gnarly pops.

Milo risked a glance at Xander, who was in an *actual* fight with Sharn, instead of this merry-go-round like Milo.

It didn't help that his chest already hurt from the distance forced between them.

"Did Poppy send you?" she shouted at Xander, who mimicked zipping their lips and throwing away the key.

Before he could watch the orc lunge, he had to turn his attention back to *his* orc, who grumbled, deep and low and dangerous, as he finally approached Milo.

"Not how I thought my night was going to go," Milo muttered, and jumped up onto the trunk of a car to avoid the orc. The car shook as the orc crashed into it, and Milo jumped onto his back, wrapping a thick forearm around his neck. He conjured the scales on his forearms to give him more leverage.

The orc spun, and Milo really should have anticipated it,

honestly. He was preparing to jump ship when a shout rang out, and everything moved in slow motion.

Sharn dug a knife out of their shoulder with a growl, and sent Xander flying.

Milo had a split second to react, jumping from his own orc's shoulders.

Instincts kicked in, and he reacted, letting the shift ripple over him in a blink. Muscles slid and bunched over his spine as he took to the air, wings flapping as he dove for Xander.

He caught their small form in his clawed hand, tucking them against his body as he slammed into a car—oops—and rolled over the top of it as the alarm began to blare. They landed on the other side and he shifted back in an instant. Xander grunted as they sat up, blinking at him wildly.

"You're fast," they remarked, drawing a dagger and risking a peek over the hood of the car, lights flashing with each obnoxious beep. They ducked back down with a grumble, chest heaving as they slid to sit.

"They're fast too, won't wait—what's wrong?" Xander asked.

Milo couldn't speak yet. He was too busy distracted by the flush lining Xander's cheeks, adrenaline making their eyes downright *sparkle*.

"Are you hurt?" they asked again, glancing him over from head to toe.

They weren't *scared* or hurt. They were *excited.*

Hunter.

I've never failed to bring back a hoard, and you know it.

Xander was a goddamned treasure hunter, and Milo kept allowing himself to forget it. They'd likely killed dragons in the past, stolen artifacts and jewels and treasures they had no right to in the first place.

Milo's anger wasn't misplaced, but his attraction, this soft spot that grew softer by the fucking hour *was.*

If Milo was smart, he'd take off with the ring, let the orcs kill Xander. The binding spell would be broken without two people to bind. There'd be one less hunter in the world, one less person to hurt the few dragons *left* in the world.

"I should just let them have you," Milo said, the words falling from his lips like a threat.

Xander blinked, stiffening momentarily before their expression shuttered. "You could. It would solve all your problems."

They're killers by nature.

Milo recalled Xander staring at the witches from across the room, in awe of the display of casual affection, gentleness.

They support a backwards system of hurt and violence.

He saw Xander, the way they'd looked all soft as they sipped tea in his kitchen.

The world—dragons—would be better off without another hunter.

A comfortable weight across his chest as sleep lost its hold, and interrupted by the absence of that weight, a grunt and a flustered excuse.

"Why don't you?" they asked.

Milo's gaze flashed to them, was met with their own intense hazel, head cocked to the side in question.

But there would also be one less Xander.

"Give me a reason not to," Milo asked, the words scraping past his lips as if he was begging. Maybe he was. He wasn't fucking heartless. Not as heartless as a hunter, in the least.

Xander's lips parted, closed. Their brow furrowed before their shoulders slumped, and Milo learned what uncertainty looked like on them.

"I've never killed a dragon," they admitted.

Milo's eyes widen, disbelief dumping over him like a pail of cold water.

"What? But you're a—"

"Yes. Yes, I know what I am!" they hissed as the orcs cursed and footsteps neared. "And I know what I'm not. A killer." They spat the word out like it left a bad taste. "Get us the fuck out of here and I'll tell you all about it."

It probably spoke volumes how quickly Milo shifted into his dragon form and scooped them up.

Xander yelled in surprise as Milo moved his wings and took to the air as naturally as breathing.

They left the orcs behind, cursing and waving their fists at them.

Once they were a comfortable distance away, Milo lifted Xander to his neck. He fought off a sneeze as their hands dragged along his sensitive scales as they adjusted their seat over his neck and clung tight.

His mind raced the whole flight, the rush of wind providing a comfortable, familiar white noise.

How is it possible Xander had *never* killed another dragon? In all their time as a Hunter of Obscure Artifacts?

Sure, they could've just been lying. Especially with their life on the line.

It certainly made no sense. All the weapons alone hinted at someone dangerous, someone not to mess with. Someone to be wary of.

His thoughts turned in circles as he flew them back to his house. From experience, he knew to stay closer to the trees than not. Before the Big Reveal, he hadn't had to worry about someone catching him on camera because the shine of his scales reflected the sky back. Built in fucking camouflage.

Now he didn't have to worry about it because if someone *did* happen to catch a flying dragon on camera, it just went viral online, pulling the *actual* trolls from their caves to the internet to talk shit.

The longer they flew, the less tense the figure on his neck

became, until Xander was—were they *petting* his scales? Milo wanted to tilt his head into it, or hell, maybe even roll over and offer his belly. But he refrained. Somehow.

It was kind of a long flight, if he was honest, especially for someone who hadn't flown a whole lot in recent weeks.

By the time his house and the lake came into view, he was flagging with exhaustion, and dipped, aiming for his spacious front yard. A gentle landing later, and he lowered his neck to the ground so Xander could climb off. They were more careful than he expected.

"Don't change yet," Xander said, holding out a hand.

Milo huffed, narrowing his eyes at them.

"Just… look at you!" Xander beamed, and Milo had to blink a few times because holy shit that *smile?*

It knocked him dumb for a few seconds, and he *did* stay in his dragon form, if only so Xander would look at him like he was magical for a bit longer.

"Your scales are fucking awesome," they said, and the words were what jarred Milo back to the present.

Yeah, his scales. His very expensive, one of a kind scales that would fetch a shiny penny on the market. No wonder Xander appreciated them so much.

He shifted back, his dragon retreating to the little cage in his chest with a huff. Milo came back into his human form with a shiver, exhaustion weighing each of his limbs.

As he blinked, the world wavered a little and—

"Hey! Milo?" Xander asked, and a strong arm wrapped around his waist, holding him up. "You're heavy," they complained, but shuffled in the direction of his front door.

The door opened without needing a key and Xander scoffed. "Don't even lock your fucking door. You stupid or something?"

"M'a dragon," he answered, as if that explained every-thing. God, he was so fucking tired suddenly, what the *fuck?*

He was out of practice. It made him feel slightly less silly about clinging to Xander like they were the only thing keeping him standing. "Flying isn't easy," he offered. "It's been a while."

"Yeah, yeah. Watch out for the—oh no." They winced as Milo knocked into one of the hall tables, sending a candle to the ground with a crash.

"Aw man, I liked the smell of that one," Milo whined as he glanced over his shoulder at the mess.

"Here, get—ugh why do you *weigh so much*," they groaned.

The bed rushed up to meet Milo head first as Xander released him, and he rolled over with a sigh.

"Are you always like this after shifting?" they asked, frowning down at him with their hands on their hips.

"Only when I've overexerted myself. Like saving your sorry ass." He chuckled at his own joke and turned his head toward them. "Hey."

They lifted their brows and tilted their head, indicated they were listening, as if they hadn't already been staring at him.

"You said you don't kill dragons. I wanna hear a bit more about that, if you don't mind."

"You gonna remember it when you wake up?"

"Yep. Probably." He hummed, eyes fluttering shut. "Maybe."

Xander laughed, low and velvety and *ooh*, that was nice. He'd like to hear it again.

"How about this," Xander began, and knelt down so they were eye level. "When we get the witch her stupid ring back and undo this binding, you show me the hoard. I'll split it with you."

"Why would I do that?" Milo asked.

"Because I'll tell the hunters you're dead. They'll get off your back. I impress the director. Everyone wins."

Milo squinted. "You'll… split my own hoard. In exchange for lying to the hunters?"

Xander smiled, patted him on the shoulder, and stood. "Yep. We can talk more about it when you wake up."

Milo wanted to reach out to Xander as they stepped away, left his line of sight, but not the room at least. His chest wasn't hurting.

Why did their story sound so familiar?

Trading hoard for anonymity and safety from the hunters?

His eyes widened slightly, but his next blink was even heavier, and despite his suspicion, his wonder, his amazement, his lids lowered.

Fuck. He'd have to ask them after he slept a bit.

10. LEGENDS AND LIES

Xander expected Milo to catch on. What they were *not* expecting was Milo to slide into the kitchen in fuzzy socks and his robe, flinging a finger in their direction, surprise on his face.

"You're The Bargain Hunter! That's why that fuckin' offer sounded so familiar! I've heard it from other dragons all over the place!"

They arched a brow, cool, calm, casual. They'd heard the title before, but it had never sounded quite so… important than when it came from Milo's lips.

"I guess that's me," they said with a shrug. They'd helped themself to Milo's electric kettle, and sipped their tea.

"You—you *help* dragons?" Milo sputtered. "But you're a… a—"

"Yes. I'm a treasure hunter, who doesn't kill dragons." The irony was not lost on Xander.

"But… why?" Milo asked, voice hazy with awe. He sat at the kitchen bar, propping his head on his hand and staring at Xander with an uncomfortable spotlight of… something.

They couldn't place it, but it made their cheeks heat all the same, and they dipped their face down to their tea for a sip.

"Do you want the whole story or the footnotes version?"

Milo nodded. "Whole story. Go."

"Want some tea?" they offered, as if this wasn't Milo's house. As if they hadn't helped themself to Milo's shower and his boxers and a soft robe, and then ignored the vise around their chest from being a room away from Milo to clean up the broken candle and make a goddamned cup of tea.

It occurred to them suddenly. "Did the uh... binding wake you up?"

"Kinda hard to sleep when it feels like someone's tightening barbed wire around your chest."

They winced, spooning a bit of the loose tea into a bag for Milo. "Sorry."

Milo cocked his head to the side. "S'alright. Was an okay nap. I feel good as new. Story time," he hinted, rolling his hand out.

They realized for the first time since this whole thing began that *they* felt in charge of the situation for once. They didn't have to hide behind a mask, pretend they were something they weren't.

"Hunters value fear. Success. So essentially, I spun a tale for them that they loved."

Milo urged them to continue, and Xander cleared their throat and tied off the tea bag. "The first time it happened was more of an accident. I was young, and got in over my head on my first mission, but failure was not an option."

"Why not? Surely everyone messes up on their first job."

"Yeah, but not everyone was raised by the director. My supervisor? Also kind of my dad." They were relieved to have something to do with their hands.

"You're pulling my tail," Milo said with a dubious expression.

"Please never say that again," Xander bit out, trying not to laugh, and grateful their back was turned.

Xander poured the hot water into his mug and watched the steam rise before they spoke again. When they turned to deliver the tea cup, they risked a glance at Milo.

He looked... enraptured, as if he was hanging onto Xander's every word.

"It wasn't a very fun-filled childhood, I'll tell you that much." *Hmm yes, childhood trauma. Let's dive right in, shall we?*

Xander leaned against the counter at their back, staring at Milo framed by his fancy counters and pretty teacups and cluttery decor that was still somehow tasteful despite the gaudy abundance.

"The pressure to succeed has been over my head for as long as I can remember. So when I got out of my depth, I panicked." Xander's throat had been in the dragon's hand, their words tinged with desperation as they'd blurted the first thing that came to mind. "Offered the dragon something more valuable than his hoard. He took the offer. Split it with me. I reported him dead, offered a few volunteered scales for proof, and off he went on his merry way."

"And they've never caught on? All these years?" A frown marred his expression as he dipped the teabag in and out of the tea.

"Nope," Xander popped the 'p' a little harder than necessary, trying to ignore the sleep creases on Milo's cheek, his mussed hair.

They were not doing a very good job.

"But you... You're..."

I'm what? "What?"

His hands fluttered helplessly. "You carry so many weapons. It's a little overkill, I mean, a whip? Really?"

"It fooled you, didn't it?" *Dress for the job you want, not the job you have, and all that.*

"Speaking of," Milo interrupted.

Xander arched a brow at him, sipped their tea and let the floral notes wash over them.

Milo leaned down, forearms resting on the bar as he sat the teacup down with a soft clink.

"You're very good at acting. Flirting with the orc. It reminded me of when we first met. You could've flirted the whole way back here, had me wrapped around your pinky. And *then* cuffed me, or made your offer."

Xander swallowed, anticipating the question.

"Why'd you fuck it all up? Why'd you cuff me when there was an easier way?"

"That was different. I couldn't just flirt my way to your hoard," Xander scoffed, ignoring the heat rushing to their cheeks.

"Why not? Take it from me, it would've worked."

Why was Milo's voice so deep and velvety? Melting across their senses like honey?

"Because—"

Xander hesitated. It wouldn't do to feed this dragon's ego, would it? Not like they could just *admit* that… the longer they spent with Milo, the less in control they felt. Beginning when Xander had watched Milo frantically decorate that stupid cake in his kitchen. Through the window, of course. From the safety of their bike. With binoculars.

Stupid dragon with his stupid pretty curls and thick arms and… how was Xander supposed to keep their cool the entire night? On the cab over?

Things would've progressed too quickly with Milo. They would've ended up shoved against the brick wall by Milo and helpless to stop it if they hadn't cuffed him when they did.

Fuuuck.

"It would've been too much—" Xander huffed, crossed their arms, tried to act nonchalant and not as if their heart was suddenly in their throat.

Milo let it go. As much as he could, anyway.

"What's the ring around your neck for?"

Surprised, Xander lifted a hand to the ring. As long as it had been around their neck, it was like a part of them, the shape of the band and the bright red jewel in its center engraved in their memory.

Xander watched as Milo observed them, his hand tightening around the tea cup as he waited for an answer.

"It's from the very first dragon I ever encountered. My first mission," they said, throat dry. "I kept it to… to remind myself of what I was doing. To be careful."

"To help the dragons?" Milo guessed, cocking his head to the side.

Xander winced. "It's still blackmail in the end. Not sure many of them would agree with you."

His hum was deep and low and questioning. "A treasure hunter who doesn't kill dragons, huh?" Milo asked, abandoning his teacup on the other side of the bar.

Xander turned to face him as he rounded the side, deep voice intimate in the quiet of the kitchen. "A treasure hunter who knows how to use knives, wears them like they plan to, but doesn't intend to hurt anyone."

They huffed out a breath, tried to school their expression into one of nonchalance. "Where are you going with this?"

"The Bargain Hunter. Here before me. In my kitchen." He backed them up all the way to the counter. Laid a hand on the flat surface behind them, effectively caging them in. "Drinking my tea and wearing my robe."

"It's a very nice robe, to be fair," Xander breathed, heart pounding in their chest at the proximity.

"It'd be nicer *off*," Milo hinted.

They froze for a heartbeat, and then Xander didn't know who moved first. If it was Milo who wrapped his arm around

Xander's waist or if it was Xander who hopped up at the same time Milo backed them into the counter.

Their arms went around Milo's neck, tugging him close and threading their fingers through his dark, soft curls, over the scales dotting the back of his neck. The strands twined around their fingers like Milo and Xander twined around each other. His hands clasped at Xander's waist and tilted them against him.

Heart pounding in their chest, in their ears, Xander angled their head, lips moving against Milo's with the same hungry curiosity they'd been wary of giving into all this time.

The question of *why* echoed louder with each passing second. Why had they waited so long to give in? Why had they not done this from the beginning? Why did Milo feel so perfect, taste so delightful against them?

Xander released his curls, broke the kiss only for a breath. Milo leaned back, amber eyes dark and wonderful as his gaze flicked over their face in question.

In answer, Xander smoothed their palms over his shoulders, down his chest before they slipped their hands beneath the robe and pushed it off. It pooled at the bend of his elbows, and they paused for a tension filled second more before Milo's lips caught Xander's again.

The dragon shimmied the robe off, leaving him bare from the waist up.

Xander spanned the new real estate with eager fingers, gliding over the scales along the back of his shoulders. The small disks somehow smooth and soft yet hard and unforgiving at the same time.

Their lips parted even more in a small gasp when they slid their hand lower, encountered the smooth roughness of the scales at his waistband. A kick of heat struck their stomach as Milo licked into their mouth, a soft groan peeling off his tongue and slipping onto their own at Xander's curious touch.

Milo broke the kiss this time, leaning back, half lidded eyes searching their expression. "I, uhm. Dragons are... We have... I'm—"

"Different. I *know*," Xander purred.

At least in theory. As a treasure hunter on the hunt for dragon hoards, they'd learned everything they could about the creatures they hunted. Including the different anatomy they were born with.

"It doesn't bother me," Xander promised before their lips quirked. "As you've probably gathered, I'm also—"

"Different," Milo echoed, with a smile. "I know."

Relief still filled them, even though they knew that Milo knew. But now they *really* knew and it was a wonderful kind of feeling, that knowledge.

Milo's hands tightened around their waist, dragged them closer as he rolled his hips and those deliciously hard scales between their legs. Xander's eyes fluttered closed, head tipping back as arousal brightened between them. His lips latched onto their neck, and Xander threaded their hands through his hair again.

"Your curls," Xander breathed. "I can't stand them. They're so pretty."

Milo paused. "Pretty?" he asked, the word whispered against Xander's throat.

Xander nodded, brushing their throat against Milo's lips. "The prettiest."

Milo groaned against them, hips curling toward the counter, pleasure rattling up Xander's spine.

So Milo liked being called pretty. *I can work with that,* they thought idly.

Milo's hands trailed up their waist, along the outside of their arms until he dug his hands into their shoulders and rid them of the robe. They only spared a moment of remorse for the way it pooled around their waist onto the counter. Now they were both bare from the waist down.

"How do you like to be touched?" Milo asked softly, pulling back to meet their gaze.

Xander's heart flipped over in their chest at Milo's question, and wondered if the swell of emotion was visible in the flicker of their eyes. Instead of answering—they'd never been asked this question before, how were they *supposed* to answer past the thump of their heart—Xander dragged his hands to their chest, chills breaking out at the warmth of his palms against their skin.

It was answer enough, and Milo tilted his head, lips meeting Xander's once again. They parted their lips and let Milo taste them, tongues flicking together as Milo's palms smoothed over their pecs, brushing over the scars. They jolted against him when he teased a nipple between his thumb and forefinger, zings of pleasure lighting up their senses.

Xander traced each scale on Milo's stomach, lips suddenly twitching as they pulled back. "Would you call these... happy scales?"

Milo blinked, lips parting before he shook his head, something fond lighting up his gaze before he cupped the back of their head and kissed them until their breath was weak.

"Ridiculous, absolutely ridiculous," Milo murmured, trailing his lips down the side of their neck again. Xander arched into the touch, chills breaking out when Milo nipped at the junction of their shoulder and throat.

"Learned from the best," they breathed in response.

Xander continued their exploration from scale to scale until they reached his waist, fingers fluttering over the band for permission.

"Go'head," Milo choked out, and Xander's lips twitched again. The effect they were having on Milo was palpable, visible, and intoxicating.

They dipped their hand below the fabric and wrapped their fingers around him with a gasp that Milo swallowed as he lifted his head back up.

The dragon *whimpered* in his throat as Xander stroked him from root to tip, the deep red scale-like texture soft and tapered and already dripping.

"You're so wet," Xander breathed against Milo's parted lips.

"For you," he whispered, hips twitching into their hand. "Holy shit."

Xander wondered if they were glowing from how bright they felt with Milo, how bright Milo *made* them feel. His hands dropped to Xander's waist, fingers hooking in the band, and Xander shuffled their hips before he could ask, urging him to tug them down.

It was awkward as they slipped and slid against the countertop, but the chuckles were perfectly endearing as Milo stripped them. They hissed, jumping at the cold of the counter before they warmed up to it. When their borrowed boxers fluttered to the floor, Xander wrapped their legs around Milo's waist and tugged him forward. He came with an *oof*, already grinning against Xander's lips.

Xander moaned into the kiss as Milo arched against them, brushing between their legs wet and warm and oh so different from anything they'd ever felt.

"Holy shit is right," Xander panted. "I want you inside me, like yesterday. Do dragons need protection?"

"It's not breeding season. No diseases," he answered. "So unless you want me to—"

Breeding season? Xander would have to ask Milo more about this later. "No, I wanna feel all of you. Fuck, *fuck*,"

Xander breathed at just the idea as Milo ground against them. They wanted all of it. They wanted him in their mouth, wanted to taste the same slick that now coated their own thighs. They wanted him any fucking way they could get him.

"I hope that nap was refreshing," Xander said, reaching between them to guide Milo between their legs. They moaned as they ground against him, the wet scales perfectly textured, overloading their senses with pleasure. "I won't be done with you for a *while*."

Milo shuddered against them, hands gripping their hips so tight they hoped he left finger shaped bruises as he rocked with them, grinding them together until Xander's breath exploded out of their chest.

"I—I've never felt... anything... *anything* this good," Xander panted.

What had they said about the dragon's ego? They couldn't find it in them to care at the moment as Milo rolled his hips against them again and again, the scales sliding between Xander's legs, stroking them higher and higher together.

They could come from this, they suddenly realized, eyes snapping open—when had they closed?—and found Milo staring at them, lips parted and something like awe sparkling in his gaze. "I wanna see it," he said suddenly. "Please, let me see you come like this."

Not even Xander was cruel enough to deny such a request from this sweet, desperate dragon, as if they weren't equally desperate. They nodded, arms wrapped around Milo's shoulders, fingers threaded through his curls—their new favorite place to hang from—as Milo dangled them over the precipice, hips working against them with a feverish pace.

He slid against them over and over, edging closer with each thrust, wet, and audibly so, their slick movements echoing around the kitchen, the filthiness of it only encouraging them.

"Come *on*," Milo pleaded, hips snapping against them in rhythm. "Please. I'll beg, just ask."

It was that image, of Milo on his knees and Xander's fingers threaded through his curls, that sent them careening over the edge, out of control as pleasure blinded them, bright crimson just like the scales of his dragon form.

"That's it, that's it," Milo whispered, words ragged as his hips slowed to a smoother, softer grind, one hand curling up to support Xander's neck as their head tilted back.

They melted toward him, letting their lips land on his, the kiss sloppy and lazy as aftershocks pulsed through their body.

After a long, drawn out moment, the gift of thought eventually returned to them as they chuckled, breaking the kiss. They leaned their head against Milo's chest.

"Now what?" Milo asked, lips twitching against their hair.

Xander barely avoided clocking his chin as they pulled back. "Now, pick which surface you wanna fuck me against first."

11. NO INTERMISSION

They tumbled backward into the bedroom, Xander barely catching them with a hand on the door frame. Milo spun them around so when they fell onto the bed, Xander landed atop him.

"Of all the surfaces in the house, you wanna start with the bed?" Xander teased. "You virgin."

"I'm a romantic, sue me," Milo said, pressing kisses against their neck, shoulders, wherever he could reach. As if he couldn't get enough.

It was downright fucking intoxicating.

Xander nodded, trying to collect their thoughts, very serious. "Yes, it was so romantic to grind me to orgasm on the kitchen counter. Very prim and proper."

Milo groaned and let his head drop to the bed. "I can't stand you."

"We're not standing right now."

Milo groaned louder, drowning out Xander's reply like a brat. Their gaze got stuck on the long line of his throat, the way his Adam's apple bobbed with his distracting noises. Xander leaned down before they could think better of it, teeth wrapping bluntly over the side of his neck.

Beneath them, Milo paused, the sound cutting off abruptly, and Xander froze, teeth digging in softly.

"Everything alright?" Milo asked, words breathy. Xander felt each word leave his throat as it flexed with his breath, and they ignored the warm twinge between their legs.

Slowly they unhinged their jaw and sat up, expression contrite. "Yep. Couldn't help it?"

"Have an oral fixation, do we?"

"Not that I know of," Xander said, their cheeks slowly heating, gaze trailing down Milo's chest. "Then again, maybe I could be convinced with a little… experimentation."

"Oh, I like the sound of that. Need a volunteer?" he teased, lips twitching.

Xander kissed the smirk right off his lips, waited until he whimpered into their mouth, sending another flare of heat through them before Milo shuffled against the bed. Xander slid against Milo, who was still hard and dripping and spreading the wetness between their legs.

"Maybe later," Xander agreed, gaze capturing Milo's as their breath went weak with a particularly delicious grind.

Milo's eyes darkened before he flipped them over, pressing Xander into the mattress. The little gasp they let out was downright embarrassing, but this dragon had the power to reduce them to nothing but need and pleasure, and—

And Xander framed his hips with their knees, arching up into him and grinding against his still hard cock. "If you don't get inside me, I think I will actually die," Xander groaned.

Milo rolled his eyes, hips grinding a smooth rhythm against Xander, a mockery of what they really wanted. "So dramatic."

Xander's growl was lost in Milo's chuckle. In retaliation, Xander dragged their nails down his sides, giddy with the way a shiver danced up his spine.

Sliding one hand between them, Xander wrapped their fingers around Milo's length, watching his eyes flutter shut. Heart pounding in their chest for *no reason, dammit,* they poised him at their entrance, clamping a lip between their teeth against the moan that threatened to spill out.

"Don't," Milo said, thumbing at their bottom lip.

They released it with a huff, wondering if Milo had any idea of the way he affected them. The way he made them… feel.

God, who are *you?*

Knees tightening around his hips, they rocked up, and Milo finally had mercy on them. He rolled his hips into them at the same time, and the tapered head of him finally slid inside.

Xander's eyes almost rolled back at the feel of him, the textured ridges of his cock brushing against every part of them.

He withdrew, teasing them with the shallowest of thrusts until Xander got their nails in his back and finally let loose the almost-whine building in their throat since the moment Milo flipped them over.

"Come on," Xander breathed, refusing to beg but almost desperate enough to.

The glide was slick and wet and perfect, and the sounds their bodies created were something out of a dream, making Xander's cheeks flush.

"You're blushing," Milo said, quick as a whip and grin just as sly. "Is it that good?"

"Shut *up,*" Xander groaned, reaching up to thread a hand through his curls and tugging his mouth down.

They licked into his parted lips, glided their tongue over the back of his teeth, reveled in the hiss of pleasure Milo shared into the kiss.

"Nah, I don't think I will," he retorted, pairing his words

with a particularly sharp thrust that pushed the breath from Xanders' lungs.

Their eyes fluttered shut. *"Fuuuck,"* they moaned. "You feel—"

They couldn't even find words to try and explain it, couldn't hold onto one thought long enough to string it together with another.

Milo fucked them like he did everything. With annoying ease and talent. Or maybe that was just a veil for the needy pleasure.

His amber eyes were darkened, curls escaping Xander's fist and dangling in his face and goddamn, even slamming his hips into them with every muscle in his body he was still so *pretty.*

"I want, I—" Xander couldn't even put the words together, the pieces splitting apart with each thrust of Milo inside them.

Urging for more, deeper, anything and everything, Xander lifted their knee toward their chest, digging the heel of their foot into Milo's side as they moved together, desperation tinging each movement.

Suddenly Milo's hand slid to the back of their thigh, notching in the bend of their knee and pressing them open even more.

Xander's mouth dropped open on a moan at the change of angle, the way Milo's thrusts quickened. Their whole body tensed with the jolt of pleasure Milo struck them with again and again.

"Yes," they panted. "Fuck, *yes.*"

"Next time," Milo breathed, and Xander lifted their gaze back open. "I wanna fuck you in the robes."

Xander's eyes widened.

"Yeah, exactly." Milo nodded, more hair slipping out of Xander's hold. "The silk... feels so good against your skin, doesn't it?" Every few words were emphasized with another kick of his hips.

They nodded helplessly, and Milo slowed, but deepened his thrusts, and Xander could feel him in their fucking throat.

"It's okay to like it. To be soft. To like soft things," he said.

Xander tipped their head back, swallowing hard against the rush of emotion Milo was fucking into them. One slow, deep thrust at a time, hips rolling smoothly into them and ending with a snap.

It forced a moan out of them every time their hips met, every time he drove into them. They broke their own fucking rule as pleas and whines and encouragement fell from their lips.

"That's it." Milo's voice broke into their litany of nonsense. "Stay with me."

"Where the fuck am I gonna go?" Xander breathed, lifting their other hand from the sheets to catch all his falling curls. They threaded their fingers at the back of Milo's head and tilted his face up to them. "I wanna see you too," they said.

Milo's eyes fluttered shut, expression scrunching as his mouth fell open, breaths spilling out between them.

Knowing Milo was just as wrecked as Xander was thrilling, was hot, hotter than expected. It was in the way his breath quickened and stuttered, the way his hips snapped and he had to fight not to rush the pace. The way his nails dug into the back of their thigh, pressing them higher and tighter and shifting the angle until Xander's breath went weak yet again.

The edge was nearing hard and fast, the opposite of the emotions bumbling around Xander's chest.

Xander glanced down between them, watched Milo drive in and out of them, the resounding pleasure blinding like the goddamned bond between them.

"Milo," they panted breathlessly, rocking their hips up into him.

Milo shifted the angle yet again, and Xander gasped as each plunge drove his scales against them.

"Good?" he asked.

Xander couldn't help their breathless laugh, gaze lifting to Milo's. "H-happy scales indeed."

His eyes rolled, before a matching chuckle bubbled up, and suddenly Xander's chest was so full they didn't know what to do. Were they going to die? They were too young for a heart attack.

But the longer they watched a matching smile curl Milo's lips, watched it fade and his lips part into agonized pleasured once again, they realized they weren't in danger at all.

The opposite. They were *enamored* with this stupid dragon and his soft clothes and his many trinkets and pretty curls.

"Fuck," they whispered, eyes widening in revelation.

Milo blinked down at them, and before he could read their expression, discover their newfound secret, they pulled him lower.

Their lips crashed together with the same urgent desperation that their hips collided.

"Oh god," they breathed into the kiss, and Milo nodded against them, lips slipping and sliding against their own in a beautiful mess.

"Yeah, I know," he said, hips canting into them over and over again.

Xander dragged their nails down the back of his neck, holding onto his shoulders, the scales hard and anchoring them to the moment. They needed *something*, otherwise they feared the edge that awaited them, feared they might slip right off the precipice and never return.

"Come on, it's okay," Milo encouraged against their lips.

Xander tasted the words right from the source, swallowed them down and as they settled, so too did the frantic edge of Xander's pleasure.

It smoothed out into something manageable.

Milo dragged them right to the horizon, bright and blinding, with each shift of his hips, each thrust, each softly murmured word that *just* kept them from floating away on it all.

Milo leaned his head down, nipped at their neck in a mimicry of how they'd bit him earlier, and whispered, "I've got you."

Fuck this dragon and his stupid soft words, and how the effect was for Xander to shatter beneath him with a shout. It should've been violent, the way the build up held them at a razor's edge, but instead…

Instead, they fell apart beneath Milo, and yet he held all the pieces together, tethered them when they felt they'd drift right away. They quivered around him, and it made each thrust that much *more*.

"Milo—Milomilomilo," they breathed, nails digging into his shoulders, pinching between his scales. They hoped they weren't hurting him, but from the way his thrusts stuttered, the way he pulsed inside them—*god, they could* feel *it*—he followed them right over the edge.

Xander clutched around him as they spiraled, following each other around and around again. They dug their nails in, groaned as the pleasure overwhelmed them. Xander curled their arm over his shoulder, threading their hand back through his hair and letting their head fall to the mattress. Above them, Milo tilted his head back, lips parting on a groan and a… puff of smoke?

He relaxed against Xander, their chests heaving together as their hearts pounded and—god, Xander wondered if Milo could fucking hear it for how hard it beat against their chest.

"Did you just breathe smoke?"

Milo's cheeks warmed impossibly redder, and he lowered Xander's leg, still shaking. Milo noticed right away, gaze lifting to Xander's with an accomplished little twitch to his lips. Xander pushed their palm against his face, turning him away playfully.

"Don't say it," they warned.

"M'kay," he agreed, flopping down next to them on the mattress, tugging them close. It was such a familiar, affectionate move that their heart thumped against their chest.

They didn't think it was in protest.

"So, the smoke?" they asked, a knowing little grin beginning to crawl across their lips.

"Yeah," he shrugged. "Happens when I get… worked up."

"So dragons *do* breathe fire," Xander mused.

"We can. It's not very pleasant. And like, destructive."

The sad way he admitted it made their chest clench with utter affection. They let the subject go, and Milo began caressing circles into their skin.

As the silence settled, they could *hear* Milo's satisfied smile grow.

"You're insufferable," Xander scolded.

Milo whined and buried his head in their neck, planting kisses along the column of their throat until their own lips finally cracked in a smile. "I know," he said.

Xander smacked his shoulder.

…and then slid their hand down his shoulder until they could tug his arm across their chest.

Once Xander had dragged them into the shower to clean up, they did less cleaning than kissing. Xander blamed it on Milo, because the dragon would *not* get his hair wet.

So, of course Xander attempted to distract Milo, tongues twining, hands refusing to drift anywhere but from where they framed his face. The kiss was stupidly soft, and Xander tried not to look too closely at the simple ease of their intimacy.

When Milo finally groaned, hands clutching at their sides, they grinned and moved to shove Milo under the spray.

But the dragon didn't budge, and Xander was only digging their hands into his chest.

"Nice try," Milo drawled, blinking at them through the mist of the spray. "I could see you plotting from a mile away."

They huffed, and Milo leaned across to kiss the frown right off their face.

"These curls take a strict routine."

Xander's huff melted into a sigh, and they leaned closer to Milo, wet skin slipping against the dragon's in a delicious friction.

They drifted their hands up his chest, over his shoulders, stroking the smooth but hard scales at his back.

"These are here all the time?"

Milo nodded. "It's my… ah, default? If that makes sense."

"Is it more comfortable?" Xander questioned, spinning Milo around to get a better look at them.

They were deep crimson, almost holographic with the way the light caught on them, just like his dragon form.

"Definitely," he answered. "I usually have some that run up the back of my forearm, but I keep those tucked away.

"What? Why?" Xander asked, reaching around him to trail their hands over his arms. "I wanna see."

"You do?" Milo sounded surprised.

"Yes! Of course. Show me?" they asked.

Milo was quiet for a long moment, and they were about to turn him back around so they could read his expression before he lifted his arm. Flexing his fingers, he breathed out long and slow before his skin rippled, the scales seeming to just… grow from his skin like petals blooming before their eyes.

More of the decadently painted scales covered the backs of his arm, some of his hand. Xander trailed their fingers gently over the surface, shivering at the unforgiving feel of them beneath their touch.

"I stopped wearing them because in the bakery… you know, the flower and sugar and frosting gets wedged in them. Kind of a pain to keep clean."

"They're pretty," Xander breathed.

Milo's breath caught, and he shut the water off abruptly.

"What—" they swallowed the question in lieu of gasping as Milo lifted them from the shower and planted them on the rug. Milo draped a towel over them and ruffled their hair, Xander's mouth dropping open at the *audacity.*

Once they were dry, Milo skipped off to the kitchen briefly and returned with two glasses of water, the deep emerald green of Xander's robe draped over his still-scaled arm. Milo had donned his own, and it flowed behind him as he walked, completely defeating the purpose of the fabric since he was still naked beneath.

Xander took their robe—*their robe, when had that happened?*—and slid it around their shoulders with a private, pleased little smile. They tugged Milo down to the bed with them after he placed their water on the nightstand.

His scales peaked out beneath the tangerine of his robe sleeve, and Xander found their hands drawn back to them, tracing each spade shaped scale like it was a work of art.

"How… how did you become a hunter?" Milo asked.

Xander's gaze lifted to his, and they continued to trace his scales, sitting cross legged and knee to knee with him on the bed. As if this were a normal evening, and they were two normal people.

"My parents kicked me out when I was fifteen," they said softly.

Milo's breath caught, disbelief shading his features, and Xander's heart gave a thump that was beginning to grow more familiar every time it happened.

"I had a few friends from school, but you can only ask for a sleepover so many times before it gets suspicious, you know? There was this queer community center, and I stayed there a few times. One of the volunteers was really cool, kept me from getting into trouble."

"When I turned sixteen, they helped me get a job at a gym. I worked nights, which was nice because I could use the showers and stuff."

Milo reached across with the hand that wasn't occupied and cupped Xander's knee. Their lips twitched at the comforting gesture, but tracing Milo's scales gave them something to focus on as they recited their history like a school syllabus.

"I became friends with the workers, some of the regulars. Caleb was the one who eventually connected me with the HOA."

"Stupid name, if you ask me," Milo muttered.

"The stupidest," Xander agreed with a nod. "I guess the director took pity on me, or something. Took me in, gave me a real place to stay, and put me in training. I was already used to exercising, because what else was I supposed to do at a gym at four in the morning, when no one else was there, y'know?"

They chuckled. "The sparring was new, and I got my ass kicked so many fucking times. Pissed me right off."

Milo huffed softly, lips curling as Xander shifted their gaze up. "You, competitive? No way," he drawled.

"Arthur was strict, regimented. We had schedules and assignments and training, the whole nine yards. It was… insane at first, coming from someone who was couch surfing for a few years with no rules. But he… Or at least it felt like he favored me over the others, even the women, though there were only a few. I wouldn't say he was soft, because Arthur doesn't do soft."

"Maybe you were impressive. I mean, you're kind of a badass, in case you missed that."

Xander rolled their eyes. "Of course *you* think that. You trip over your own feet."

Milo barked out a laugh that made Xander's chest all light and bubbly. "You are the *definition* of a badass."

He was right, and Xander knew it, but that didn't make accepting the compliment any easier.

"After my parents… I was nervous, and Arthur was even more strict in his own way. But hunters, we all kind of wear the same thing? So it was easier, in a way. Of course, there were a few dense ones who didn't get the memo." Their gaze flicked to Milo. "But I had permission to *educate* them."

"With your fists," Milo clarified, smile twitching at his lips.

"Of course. Had to make sure the lessons stuck, y'know? Anyway, the hunters respected me for it, and it wasn't very long after when I realized they'd become my family, and for the most part… let me charter my own course." Xander frowned. That sounded kind of sad, didn't it? "I mean, they're the reason I had access to the healthcare I needed. They're all I have."

So maybe the hunters weren't *all* as accepting as they would be in a perfect world, but the ones who mattered to Xander were. Like Caleb, who'd mentored them through training, who'd laughed with them late into the night to help Xander pick a name.

Their lips twitched at the memory. "I started going by Xander because—"

"You don't have to tell me, you know," Milo interrupted softly. "Dead names are dead for a reason. I understand that, and you don't owe me anything."

Be still their heart. Milo's eager acceptance made their chest go all fizzy again, and that's not even where Xander had intended to lead the conversation. "Are you sure you don't wanna know? It's kinda funny."

Milo narrowed his gaze. "Okay, fine. Only if you want to."

Xander couldn't help it. They leaned forward and nipped Milo's lips out of sheer affection.

"I chose Xander because it started with an X."

Milo blinked softly.

"You know, X marks the spot."

A certain lightness burst in their chest at the way Milo's mouth parted slightly, disbelief bright on his features. "You're pulling my—you're kidding me."

"I'm a treasure hunter. It's appropriate, isn't it?"

Milo's chest bounced as he chuckled. "A little on the nose."

Xander couldn't help the laugh that bubbled out alongside Milo's, and in moments they were in tears from the silliness. "Have you ever even needed a treasure map?"

"What?" they cackled. "No. Not once. That's what GPS is for!"

They howled with laughter, the sounds of their unfiltered joy bouncing around the room, until they laid back in the bed and clutched their stomachs and wiped tears away.

Xander's cheeks hurt, and they prodded at the sore muscles before letting the giggles finally fade.

This moment, this night, was so perfect, Xander never wanted it to end.

Milo pursed his lips. "Thanks for sharing all that with me," he murmured. "I'm a little annoyed it endears the hunters to me. Just the slightest."

Xander snorted. "Oh, they're still a bunch of assholes. Like frat boys but with weapons and even more inflated egos. Most of them think they're doing some grand, almost holy *thing*, killing dragons and taking hoards for no reason than because they like the rewards. Greed, all that." Xander waved a hand in the air, and for once, the pinch in their chest when they thought of everything the hunters did didn't go away.

"But…?" Milo questioned.

How did this dragon know them so well already?

"But…" Xander continued. "They're the first people in my life that accepted me for who I am. We're a family, in a way. I don't know where I'd be without them."

The sheets rustled as Milo's hand sought theirs, and their fingers twined together. "I'm glad they were there for you when you needed them."

They tried to ignore the elephant in the room. Ignored the weight on Xander's chest as they tried to think of what came *after*.

They still didn't have Milo's hoard, and Xander didn't know if they had it in them to ask for it. What were they going to do when their time ran out?

Because they… *This* had an expiration date, ticking closer with every moment that passed. Arthur would be ringing Xander, demanding to know if they had succeeded. If they failed, Arthur would be annoyed, but he'd get over it.

Would Xander?

"Hey," Milo said softly, turning toward them in the bed

and placing a hand on their cheek to pull their gaze to his own. "Don't go there."

Xander nodded, shifting their thoughts before the weight of it could crush them.

"What did you do in Hell?"

Milo's lips twitched.

"Glorified courier. Once cell phones were invented, our jobs became obsolete, and it was so fucking hot down there. Lucifer isn't always the most hands on guy, especially in the last few hundred years or so. We got out when we could, and I seriously don't think he's ever noticed."

"You were Hell's pigeons?" Xander teased.

Milo rolled his eyes. "Yeah. What makes it worse is that demons have wings too, so they could've just gotten one of them to do it. Gold looking bastards, from their heavenly feathers falling off."

"So demons are… a thing?" Xander wasn't sure why this surprised them, especially not when every other supernatural creature existed. "Why didn't they come out during the Big Reveal?"

"They probably figured the idea of Heaven and Hell actually existing was too much for humans to handle. Fairies and nymphs? Sure. Demons from Hell? Bit bigger of a pill to swallow."

"I can see that," Xander agreed. "And angels?"

"They're too good to mix with humans. Snobby bunch, to be honest."

Xander snorted at that, wondering if it was some great offense to talk that way about literal angels from Heaven. Then it spiraled into something more; where would Xander go, after their spins around the sun were up?

They'd never thought about it. Imagined all the lying and betraying they did probably hadn't earned them any brownie points. They winced, and turned their thoughts elsewhere.

Milo's thumb stroked over their cheek. "I'm sorry you had it so rough growing up. Parents are shit."

Xander shrugged. "It's okay. I got over it. Found people who... care about me." They choked on the word *love*, because the Hunters of Obscure Artifacts weren't really the *loving* bunch. But they laughed and teased each other and sparred and helped patch one other up after more difficult hunts. That was love, right? As long as Xander did their job, they were part of that family.

"Can I tell you something? And you not take offense?" Milo asked, voice soft and private, this moment belonging to them only. Xander pushed thoughts of the hunters away.

"Maybe," they whispered.

"I wanna... I want to take care of you," Milo admitted. "Not because I feel sorry for you, or because I think you need it. But because it's nice to be taken care of. I want to give that to you."

Their breath caught, heavy in their chest and weighed down with the realness of the emotions clogging their throat.

"How do you plan to do that?"

"Well, first... how tired are you?"

It *had* been a big day, but Xander was reluctant to even entertain the thought of falling asleep. That would mean the night ended.

"Not at all," they lied.

Milo's lips twitched, as if he could hear it in their voice, but his smile was soft and fond and something even *more* blazed out of his eyes as he sat up, captured their hand, and pulled them off the bed toward his closet.

"You like the robe, yeah? Better than the poncho?"

The light flicked to life upon their entry, and Xander greedily took in all the colors of Milo's wardrobe. "Yeah. The robe is my favorite."

The way Milo's eyes softened, revealing the utter fondness beneath, was more than they were ready to see. Especially because an echo of the same emotions bumbled around their chest.

"Try this," Milo said, finally turning away to run his hands across the shoulders of all his hangers, until he plucked something dark red from the rack. It was a *velvet* button up and Xander drifted their fingers over the soft material. "You look... really fucking good in a button up," Milo explained. "Indulge me."

Xander began to wonder if that was such a terrible idea after all.

12. MISSION COMPLETE

The veil of sleep lifted from Milo slowly, and he floated in that warm, soft in-between, visions of his dream escaping him. Xander must've been exhausted, what with all the running around Milo's head through the night.

He tried to will himself back to sleep, eager to feel more of Xander's soft touch, their warm lips against his skin, traveling further and further down his body until—

Milo jolted at the firm hand wrapping gently around his hardening cock, eyes flashing open as the dream disappeared for something much better. Reality.

A sound pushed out of his throat, unbidden, as his fingers clenched around the sheets. With a turn of his head he confirmed that Xander was no longer lying beside him. He swallowed, lifted the sheet, and found Xander staring up at him from between his legs.

"Good morning," they said, dragging a kiss along his length.

"It's about to be," Milo croaked out, voice still heavy with sleep. "Jesus."

"That's not my name," Xander retorted, lips shining with the slick of his cock.

Milo's lips parted, but no sound came out, beyond weak for the horny creature beneath the blanket, stroking him slowly.

"I wanted to do this last night," Xander continued against his thigh, nipping at the sensitive skin, and god, were they always this talkative in the morning? Milo loved it.

…liked it. *Like*. Totally casual liking.

"Didn't get a chance to—" Yeah, because Milo was too busy ripping that velvet button up off them with his teeth, "—but I figured we've got time before we leave for the witches, right?"

What was he thinking about? Milo's thoughts were like sand slipping through his fingers.

Xander smirked at him. "That's what I thought."

Any response Milo could've conjured up fled his mind the moment Xander parted their lips around him. His eyes went wide, and Milo grabbed the pillows to stack beneath his head as lightning shot down his spine to kick him in the stomach.

He threw the sheet back, ignoring it as it fluttered to the end of the bed in favor of watching Xander. They teased at the tapered head of him, tongue flicking along the ridges, encouraging more arousal to well. Their head bobbed as they swallowed, and a choked noise spilled from Milo's lips, eyes threatening to flutter shut. But he didn't let them because the sight between his thighs was so much better than anything he could've imagined in a dream or otherwise.

"You felt so good inside me," Xander suddenly said, pulling off with a pop. They stroked him, and Milo's hips arched up into their touch of their own accord. "I could spend all day down here, exploring you."

They laid their arms over his thighs, holding him down as they resumed tasting him.

The hot, wet heat of Xander's mouth was heavenly. The

eagerness they swallowed him with, the way they went a little further each time.

What they couldn't take, they wrapped their fingers around, following their mouth and tightening their grip until Milo bucked up against them with a broken noise.

"Sorry, sorry—" he panted as they pulled away, a shimmering line of slick connecting their bottom lip to the tip of his cock until it popped.

Heat swelled even hotter in him at the sight.

"I didn't mean to. Don't stop," he begged, reduced to putty in their hands after less than a handful of moments.

"I don't plan on it," Xander rasped. "I'm having quite a good time down here. And you?"

They didn't give him a chance to answer before they wrapped their lips around him again, sucking hard and swallowing around him until Milo shouted, hands flying to the back of their head, fingers twining through their hair. He didn't push or pull, simply held on for the ride and let Xander begin to ruin him.

They took a little more on each downward stroke, lips glossy with his arousal. It coated the hand that stroked him until they flattened it against his pelvis.

Milo bit his tongue as he bumped the back of their throat, as they swallowed around him. His eyes fluttered shut at the overwhelming pleasure flooding his senses.

But then the bliss was gone as Xander pulled off, their panting breaths brushing against the head of him, and Milo dropped a hand from their hair.

"Don't be quiet," Xander scolded, resting their head against his thigh.

Fuck, they were magnificent. He brushed a strand of hair away from their face, and they nudged into his touch.

"I wanna hear how good I'm making you feel," they said with a slow stroke of his length.

Milo pulsed in their grip and nodded. "Okay. Okay, yeah," he said super eloquently.

"Impressive vocabulary," Xander teased.

Rolling his eyes, Milo parted his lips to say… something, probably, most definitely, but damned if he knew what it was as Xander took him into their mouth again.

A mix between a grunt and a moan was pulled out of him, and the fingers of his left hand tightened in Xander's hair.

There was a desperation to their movements, not in their pace, but in the reverence they tasted him with. As if they knew—as well as he did—that their time was limited, that they needed to steal, hoard every piece of one another they could find.

Their gaze darted up to Milo briefly, and his abs tensed with the force of arousal that struck him. They spread their hands along his hips, holding him down as they took him deeper and deeper, eyes fluttering shut as ecstasy shimmered up his spine.

This time when he bumped the back of their throat, they didn't hesitate before swallowing him more still. Xander hummed around him, and Milo shouted, jerked as his fist tightened in their hair, but Xander's firm hold on his hips kept him from forcing himself further into the bliss of their mouth.

"Oh fuck—just like that, ah—" Milo gasped out.

A long, agonizing moment passed by them as Xander's rhythm steadied, as they bobbed their head lower with every pass, taking more and more of him until pleas and whines both were spilling from Milo's lips, until his hand was fisted in the sheets so tightly he feared he'd rip them.

He'd just buy new ones, he decided.

In that moment, nothing existed outside the two of them. The hot perfection of Xander's mouth, the drag of their tongue, the hum in their throat when their lips finally brushed the base of him.

Milo snapped his eyes open—he can't *believe* he let them close, missed even a second of this—and his entire body flushed white-hot. Xander was staring up at him, waiting for him to see. When their gazes met, Xander slowly bobbed, lifting their head up, scant, shiny inches of him appearing before Xander swallowed him again, lips stretched around his length.

"Fuck, look at you," he breathed, cock pulsing against their tongue. "I'm not—I can't—Xan*der*," he groaned, hand lifting from the sheets helplessly. He didn't know where to place it, and let it rest on his thigh uselessly, nails digging into his own skin.

"I'm gonna come," he panted, as Xander's rhythm returned, as they swallowed around him, throat fluttering.

Xander dragged their hand lower from Milo's hip to his hand, and Milo threaded their fingers together as they renewed their efforts.

Milo tensed, pleasure right on the cusp of burning him up, cindering him to ashes and hoping that Xander was there to scoop them up and make him whole again.

"Xander, I—fuck, Xander, *Xander*," he warned, groaned, shouted hoarsely as Xander sucked hard, shoving him right into the flames with no mercy.

The pleasure was scorching, unending, delicious, like nothing he'd ever fucking felt before. His hand tightened around Xander's fingers, flexing, and Xander squeezed right back as Milo spilled down their throat. They took every-thing, swallowing around him beautifully, only the slightest few drops escaping out the side of their lips, down their chin.

Milo's pulse was loud in his ears by the time Xander finally released him, and even though his entire body was no better than a bowl of noodles, he pulled Xander up to him and wrapped his arms around their waist.

He kissed them, because words were next to impossible, and tasted himself on their tongue, drawing his lips to the corner of their mouth and lower until no trace of himself was left. But then a salty drop caught against his tongue and he pulled back, finding their hazel eyes swimming in a pool of tears.

"Xander," he breathed, alarm striking his chest. "What's wrong, did I—"

"No," they rasped, voice rough. "You didn't do anything." But more tears spilled out and they kept coming, and Milo couldn't do anything but tuck them against his chest and wait for it to end.

"You wanna talk about it?" Milo asked after excruciating moments of softly whispered comfort.

"That was just..." they hesitated, swallowing so loudly Milo could hear it. "It was really *sweet.*"

Milo's lips twitched, heart caving in, emotion welling so intensely he had to swallow around it. "I literally just came down your throat, but I'm so glad you think I'm sweet," Milo teased, hoarse.

Xander snorted, slapping him on the chest, and nuzzled their face into his neck.

"You held my hand," they sniffled.

Milo's heart gave a rather fatal thump in his chest. This was it. This was how he died. Heart swelling with affection so grand it popped like a balloon.

How had he ever thought this soft, awe inspiring creature was some murderous hunter?

How was he supposed to let them go at the end of this? How was he supposed to decide which part of his hoard he gave them?

He could give them every robe he owned. Every velvet

shirt. Two of each poncho. Every fucking trinket or shiny piece of jewelry.

But none of it fucking mattered because they already had the most vital part of him right in their hands and they didn't even know it.

Milo wanted to keep Xander, not like another trinket to collect, but because they deserved the softness and care only Milo could give them. They could play dress up every single day, and Milo could introduce them to the claw foot tub and all the frilly scents he loved. He could buy them new clothes just to rip them off later, just because he *could*.

With a shuddering breath, Milo realized he'd give his whole hoard away if only so he wouldn't have to let Xander go.

It was with that shattering revelation that they finally crawled from the bed. Showered—well, made Xander come in the palm of his hand while the water rained down on them —dressed, and made their way to the witches.

The ride was silent, every minute ticking by louder than the last. Milo held Xander's hand between them on the bucket seat, only because he was helpless not to. He stroked over the back of their hand, thumb tracing the warmth of their fingerless gloves as he counted down the minutes they had left.

The trek through the woods wasn't as perilous when what awaited them on the other side was worse than any trap they'd find beneath the leaves.

If Xander held his hand just as tightly, neither of them mentioned it.

Poppy waited for them by the boulder this time, and Milo tried not to mourn the extra moments with Xander he'd just lost.

"I can't thank you enough," Poppy said with a grin, eyes

latching onto the ring as soon as Xander pulled it out of their pocket. They held it back out of reach.

"Eh," they tsked. "Undo the bond."

The words sounded forced even to Milo, and his chest heaved.

The witch rolled her eyes, waved her hand, and that same blinding light filled the forest for a split second before there suddenly seemed like twice as much room in Milo's chest.

Xander shared a glance with him, and without a word, Milo stepped back, further and further and hating every inch, but realizing there was no barbed wire wrapping around his chest as they increased the distance between them.

"Pleasure doing business with you," Poppy said, smug as Xander handed over the ring.

"Good luck with the proposal," Milo said, waving to the witch as she disappeared around the rock.

"Well, that was easier than expected," Xander said dryly, a huff of a laugh spilling out.

The walk back to the car was even more difficult. It was as if the witch hadn't removed the bond at all with the way his chest cramped with every mile they grew closer to the house.

By the time they parked in the driveway, Milo's throat was tight.

Neither of them moved. The silence was loud, oppressive.

They both knew what came next.

"Tea?" Milo offered. Because he was weak.

Weak for this creature in the car next to him, who was just as tense as he was.

Did they dread this next part as much as he did? Was their chest clamped tight like his? Were they as reluctant to peel their fingers away from the gearshift as he was?

"Tea sounds good," they whispered.

I hate this.

I want to keep you.

Don't go.

But instead of letting any of his forbidden thoughts spill past the fortress of his lips, he opened the door and led Xander inside.

13. DECISIONS

Xander was on Milo the second he opened the door to his place again.

Their lips crashed together as Milo shut the door behind him, and Xander pushed him against it.

Funny, now that the binding was gone, they wanted to be closer to Milo than ever.

He hummed into the kiss, hands sliding from Xander's waist to cup the back of their head. Xander pushed their leather clad palms beneath his jacket and up to his shoulders, then down his arms until Milo finally let the fabric drop to the floor.

Fisting their hand in Milo's shirt, they marched backward and tugged him along, giving into the giddy smile that curled their lips.

"You know," Milo said, voice wavering before dipping down to press his lips to Xander's. "The binding is gone. We could even sit in separate rooms if we wan—"

"Shut up," Xander said, pushing him down onto the couch.

They tossed a leg over his lap and sat.

"Shutting up."

They reveled in the bliss of being with Milo. Nothing had

ever felt so natural, so easy, and they dipped their head down to kiss him again.

Milo's hands lifted to frame their waist, tugging them down against him, grinding up at the same time.

Fuck.

"That's the idea here," Milo retorted, and Xander realized they'd spoken aloud.

Two could play at that game, Xander thought with a smug little grin, and threaded their fingers through Milo's curls, tipping his head back.

This was easy. This was perfect. This didn't make dread curl in their stomach.

I hate this.

The long line of his throat called to them, and Xander dipped down for a taste. All the while, Milo pushed and pulled them in his lap, sending zings of pleasure skittering up and down their senses.

"Can't believe I was missing out on this all along," Xander panted.

Milo pulled back and arched a brow at them in question.

Xander kept teasing. "I mean, if all dragons are equipped as nicely as—ah—you," they hinted.

The growl that tumbled out of Milo's lips made them *melt* against him, and they dragged his shirt up, exposing the smooth, shiny scales that lead beneath his waistband.

His touch was possessive, fingers pressing into their skin like he didn't want to let them go.

Keep me.

Milo dragged them closer, tugged them down over his scales and Xander could feel the texture through their thin pants. Their eyes fluttered shut, and they dipped their head down to Milo's shoulder.

"It makes —ah, fuck—no sense why there are scales... right here," Xander panted.

"Does it have to make sense?" he asked, fingers tightening around Xander's waist.

He dragged them over the patch of scales along his happy trail, shiny and textured and—

"It feels good?" Milo asked, voice deep and smooth and not at all like he was riding the edge alongside them. Xander dragged their nails along the back of his neck and nodded.

"So good." Each nudge of their hips over him sent them a little closer.

Their breath exploded out of them as Milo ground his hips up and dragged them down at the same time. Tilting their head back, they chased the pleasure in Milo's lap. His lips latched onto Xander's neck, sending shivers along their skin, teeth nibbling in the dip of where their neck and shoulder met.

Xander's body tensed as they neared the edge a little more with each grind, each drag of Milo's mouth, each whispered encouragement that dripped from his lips.

Don't let me g—

Their lashes parted, and as their gaze turned down to Milo, eager to soak up every moment of him they could, imprinting him into their memory, movement from the other side of the window caught their attention.

A figure dressed in all black, slinking along the side of the house.

Xander froze, and Milo paused with them. His gaze latched onto Xander's, found the alarm bright in their expression as they leaned down to his ear and whispered. "The hunters are here," they said hoarsely, something close to panic unraveling inside them. "I need you to get out and very *literally* fly away from here. Please."

There was no telling what the hunters would do to him.

"What?" he practically growled. "There's no wa—"

A booming thud and a rush of footsteps came from the entrance.

Xander's instincts reared as they reached down to their thigh harness and pulled a knife free, shifting their weight and pulling their leg back over Milo's lap to slam to the floor silently, facing the doorway as familiar faces piled in.

Their heart pounded in their chest, confusion swirling as their fingers twitched over the hilt of the knife.

"You'll be dead before it leaves your hand," the director said.

The small crowd—Xander could still take them, probably—of hunters parted, and a familiar head of salt and pepper hair made his way to the front.

The pause was so tense Xander's blade could have cut it.

The supervisor took in their surroundings—the trinkets on the wall, the lavish furnishings, the two coffee cups on the kitchen bar, their discarded jackets—before finally eying the ruffled shirt on Xander's frame, and the equally ruffled Milo. Scales had begun to crawl up his arm, his taloned hand flexing.

Now was *really* not the time to find his protective instincts so hot.

"Surely when I said to tell me if you've ever been compromised, you realized it included *fucking* the dragons too, yes?"

Xander ground their teeth together. He made it sound so... cheap.

As if Xander would do something so reckless for a few moments of pleasure?

They kept their mouth shut, and felt more than saw Milo's attention snap to them.

"Did you even secure the hoard, or did you fuck that up too?"

"I haven't completed the mission," Xander growled.

"Correct. I'm not here about *this* mission," he glared at the dragon, at their compromised state. "But this certainly is something to address as well."

Xander froze to their very core, mind blanking of everything except the secrets they'd kept hidden for so long.

"Then why the fuck are you here?" Xander asked, as if they had any leverage in this situation.

"Take him somewhere else. I need to talk to Xander. Alone," the director snapped.

At the bark of his tone, the hunters moved.

Xander knew it would just dig their own grave deeper, but they turned their head and slowly shook it at Milo.

"Don't fight," they mouthed.

It took everything in them not to leap at the first hunter to wrap his hand around Milo's arm, tugging him from the couch.

More of those fucking cuffs were slapped around his wrist, and his scales dissolved back into his arm. Milo, eyes wide and confused, stared at them as he was pulled from the room.

Fuck.

Xander sat on the couch, stretched out, nonchalant, as if this wasn't the most mortifying situation Xander could've landed in. As if that panic wasn't in full bloom, making them have to work to keep their breath in check because their heart was pounding beneath the cover of their chest.

They stared up at Arthur as if it was just another day. Not as if their heart was thumping, fear and dread and nerves swirling into a dangerously dizzy rush.

"What happened to trusting me?" Xander asked.

"I'll be asking the questions here," he snapped, and began pacing the length of the floor. "Out," he commanded, and the hunters left the sitting room, shutting one half of the parlor doors to offer them the illusion of privacy.

Each angry step was a thump on the rug; felt like another nail in their coffin.

"How long has this been going on?"

Betraying the hunters or fucking a dragon?

"Does it matter?"

He huffed. "I know you prefer not to be seen as a woman in my ranks," he began, and Xander froze. Disbelief flashed through them, scalding and impossible as his words sank in. They ground their teeth, hands clenching over the edge of the cushion. "So for you to use your... wiles to secure hoards—"

"Excuse me?" Xander snapped, sitting forward on their seat and capturing Arthur's attention. That hadn't been a slip of tongue, a mistake. No, his words were dripping with distaste. Is that really what he saw them as? After all this time? What did they even say to that? Their chest was tight, mind racing and stomach churning with devastation, all in the momentary pause of their words as they tried to corral their thoughts.

As Arthur stared at them, allowing the interruption, disappointment was clear on his face.

They swallowed back the hurt, breathed through the betrayal that Arthur wielded more deftly than any knife he could plunge into their stomach, and narrowed their gaze.

"What you think of me is your own burden. But you damn well know that is *not* how I secure the hoards. This was just a—"

"A lapse in judgment better be the phrase that follows," he said, tone scathing. "You were caught up in the moment. Let it get the best of you. *That* is an acceptable offense. *That* is something I can fight for you with."

Fight for me? Xander barely refrained from scoffing. How did he expect to *fight for them* if he couldn't even respect who they were?

Xander didn't say anything, because they both knew that wasn't true. Xander couldn't even find it in them to lie about Milo, or to lessen the... attachment they had to him. They weren't going to do that to Milo.

Arthur must have read that in their gaze.

"After everything I've done for you..." he whispered, shaking his head, disappointment clear as day.

And still only a slight less painful than Arthur's apparent view of them.

"I made a home for you," he hissed, stepping forward and dropping down onto the ottoman. "I saved you," he insisted.

Xander finally looked away, throat growing tight, sinuses burning. Because despite it all... "I know," Xander admitted.

"I—"

"Pulled me off the street. Gave me somewhere to go." They'd heard it a hundred times, whispered it to themself at night and let the guilt fester as they betrayed the hunters again and again.

"I would say I made them respect you, the other hunters, but we both know that's not true. *You* made them respect you. Because you're *good* at this. Better than any other hunter I've known."

Xander wanted to laugh, or cry. Maybe even scream a little. Because he wouldn't be saying that if he knew exactly *how* Xander had become so successful. If he knew what Xander had been doing behind his back.

Xander wasn't a hunter at all.

But that didn't mean hunters weren't their family.

It wasn't perfect; no family was. But once they'd realized they could trust Xander, they'd respected them, trained and fought alongside them, welcomed them into the fold.

"Fuck," Xander whispered, wiping at their eyes. Crying was the *last* thing they needed right then.

Arthur was right. He'd taken them in, created a home for

them. Provided the opportunity for them to fully realize who they knew they always were. The hunters had accepted Xander once they began transitioning, hadn't even teased them about it.

Once again it dawned on Xander how… sad that sounded. But it was leagues of improvement from the situation in which the hunters had first found Xander.

"How could you do this? Dragons are the enemy," the director said, voice low.

Xander didn't *know*.

But Xander didn't hate Milo. Couldn't even imagine it. But they also couldn't admit it, not to Arthur's face. He would probably laugh, or cry, or just kill them both outright.

Xander didn't know which one would be worse.

"Are you going to turn your back on your family for a *dragon*?"

Was that what they thought Xander was doing? Turning their back on them?

"You can't have it both ways," he said, voice sad.

Xander swallowed, lifted their gaze back to him. "I'm sorry," they whispered.

He flattened out his sullen expression. "What happened on your other missions?"

"What?" Xander asked, their hopelessness fading in the light of their confusion.

"Have you been protecting them? Hiding them away?"

Their heart leapt into their throat. How did he know?

Arthur's lips thinned. "Two years ago, you were on the case of a dragon named Lionel. You brought us his scales, a sizeable hoard, like usual. No one questioned you."

Xander waited for the other shoe to drop. "Until two days ago, when Jeffery was tasked with collecting a hoard from a dragon named Alice."

What did this have to do with anything? *Where* was this goin—

"Lionel's wife."

The floor fell out from beneath them.

"Jeffery was killed in battle. He was sent after one dragon, and found two. One of which was supposed to be dead."

Xander's breath exploded out of them. They *knew* Jeffery.

The dragon was supposed to *disappear.* Why would he be so stupid as to—

No. This was on Xander. Jeffery was dead because of what they'd done.

Arthur must have read the devastation in their eyes.

"We have two options. Come with me."

Xander tried to calm their racing heart, and followed Arthur numbly, mind turning over and over again.

This is my fault.

He led them out the side door and onto the lawn.

Their pulse sped up at the sight of Milo, stomach dropping at those fucking cuffs again.

Oh god. Oh fuck.

This was real. What was *this*?

This was all happening because of Xander.

The hunters had given Xander *everything* and they repaid them by... by killing one of them.

Milo's hazel gaze lifted to Xander's and the whole world stopped for a moment. His gaze raked them from head to toe, as if making sure they were uninjured.

The director did not look pleased as he exchanged a few words with Caleb, who shot wide eyes in their direction.

Xander felt suffocated under the tension in the air. The attention of every hunter was locked on them, judgment and betrayal burning from their gazes as they stared at Xander.

The ground was crumbling beneath their feet one pebble at a time. They couldn't breathe.

"As I was saying," the director addressed the hunters, motioning Xander forward, a few feet away from Milo. "There has been some speculation," he began, pacing once again with his hands clasped behind his back. "Rumors. Whatever you'd like to call it. Today, I'd like to put them to rest."

He came to a stop before Xander, and held his hand out. In his palm rested a dagger, and Xander's stomach dropped. Panic bubbled, and they lifted their gaze to Milo.

"Look at me." His tone pulled Xander's gaze back to Arthur with a snap. "Kill him."

Xander's heart stopped. They didn't breathe, couldn't, their mind still stuck on the demand.

"Prove that you're one of us. That you're a hunter like you've claimed all these years."

You killed Jeffrey.

"Well?" Arthur pressed, expectant. His hand slipped around Xander's, curled their palm around the handle so tight the leather of their gloves squeaked. Xander's gaze finally lifted from the shine of the blade. Arthur stared at them, demanding, *pleading* without saying a word. Kill Milo or...

Or.

Xander's actions resulted in the death of a hunter. That was unforgivable.

He's just a dragon.

The familiar voice in their head said the words, words that Xander had repeated a hundred times over, and yet it didn't ring any truer than it ever had.

What would happen after? Xander would be forced to give up all the dragons they'd helped over the years. To undo all the good they'd tried to do.

A means to an end.

Arthur huffed a breath, palmed their shoulder, and pushed them forward.

Xander stopped just a foot away from Milo, and the other hunters backed up, were watching from the semi circle of judgment they created. A jury, and Xander was guilty.

It offered them the illusion of privacy when they had anything but, and Xander's gaze bore into Milo.

"Fancy meeting you here," he whispered.

Tears rushed to Xander's eyes, but they *refused*, choked them back and bit into their wobbling lip.

Milo lifted a hand to their face, cupping their cheek in a warm palm. The clank of chains hung between them, brushed against the shirt Xander still wore. Milo's shirt.

"It's okay," he said softly.

Xander blinked at him. "What?" Their heart sank.

"Do it."

Xander's lips parted, but no sound came out. They couldn't make their voice work.

Resolve glittered darkly in Milo's gaze, flicking over Xander's face. "It's okay if it's you."

Oh... fuck.

The tears they'd swallowed returned with a vengeance and Milo caught one with his thumb, brushing their cheek dry. "I know what they mean to you," he said, quieter. As if they were alone, not with a crowd of hunters demanding...

They couldn't even put words to it, couldn't even *think* it.

And Milo was just... alright with this?

Xander nudged their cheek into his palm, closed their eyes. Tried to imagine it.

Saving their own hide, thrusting the blade into Milo, feeling his skin give way beneath the sharp edge. It was the easiest way out. Prove to Xander's family that they belonged, that they hadn't spent the last several years lying about how they acquired dragons' hoards. Betraying them. Resulting in one of their own's death.

But what would they have to sacrifice in its place?

They let their eyes drift open, stared at Milo, the resignation in his gaze alongside something too big to put a name to. Something they hadn't had time to explore, something that was being cut short because—because life wasn't fucking fair. Because Xander was stupid.

Arthur was right. They couldn't have it both ways.

They couldn't protect dragons, help them, and claim to be a hunter.

But could they kill them? Could they kill Milo?

Milo, who'd shown them nothing but softness and kindness and acceptance from the beginning?

Xander stretched up, curled a hand around the back of his neck and crushed their lips to Milo's, ignoring the surprised gasps of the hunters around them.

"What if you mean more?" Xander whispered, almost afraid to give the words breath.

His eyes widened, shock and more of that *too big too fast too much* drifting through his dark orbs.

Xander kissed him again, released the hold on his scaled neck, trailed it down his arms, the cuffed hands that were holding onto the collar of Xander's shirt. They pulled his hands free, cupped them briefly before releasing him altogether.

Then they stepped back and adjusted their grip on the hilt of the blade.

With a sigh, they threw it into the ground, watching it wobble with the force of the throw.

"I've been a hunter for almost fifteen years," they admitted, forcing their voice to be strong, to reach the hunters gathered around them to watch the spectacle. "I've brought in *billions*, and I've done it without spilling a single. Drop. Of blood."

More gasps. Xander had never considered themself a theater gay, but oh god, the drama? Their heart raced with it.

"I won't start now."

Arthur's harsh curse rang out, and Xander didn't fight it when two hunters clasped each of their arms in a tight grip and pulled them away. "Take Xander back to HQ," Arthur spat. "I'll decide what to do with you later."

Milo's expression was still downright shocked, and Xander tried not to be hurt by it as they were led to a black official looking SUV.

Casual and conspicuous, just the hunter style.

Xander was shoved into the vehicle, their wrists zip tied by a familiar face. They'd grown up with this person, Caleb, and now he couldn't even look them in the eyes.

"This isn't right," Xander hissed. "And you—"

"Shut up. If you know what's good for you, shut the hell up," he insisted, and then shoved Xander further into the car before slamming the door.

Arthur stalked up to the vehicle, exchanged terse words with the man that Xander had trusted.

The windows were tinted dark, but Xander could barely make out the sight of Milo being rushed back into the house.

What the hell were they going to do to him?

Xander swallowed down nausea at the thought and slammed their head into the seat.

Fuck.

14. FAMILIAL TIES

Xander jostled as the driver, Ralph, hit another pothole too harshly, wincing as their head bumped the roof of the car.

"Do you fucking mind?" they snapped.

"No, not at all. Why do you ask?" Ralph responded dryly.

Grinding their teeth together, Xander glared at Caleb, the one who'd put the zip ties on, the one sitting in the passenger seat. "Caleb, why can't you drive? At least you know how to stay in the lines."

The hunters ignored the jab. *Hunters.* As if these three men weren't people who'd been around Xander their whole life, since they were first picked up off the street.

"Where are we going, anyway?" Xander asked, hardening their voice. This wasn't in the direction of the temporary headquarters they'd established at the beginning of the mission.

The two men in the front exchange a glance that did not bode well for Xander. They refrained from answering.

Xander glanced to the last guy, on their right in the back-seat with them. His name was Ian, and Xander hadn't ever worked very closely with him. In fact, Ian hadn't left any kind of memorable impression on Xander.

Before Xander could decipher what the hell their silence meant, the shrill ring of a phone interrupted the silence.

Caleb held the slim device to his ear, listened for a moment before scoffing. "What do you mean he says he doesn't have a—well, what did Arthur say?"

A long pause, voice rising on the other end of the line.

Xander was only able to pick up a single word. *Scales*.

Dread filled them, thick and dark and heavy.

"If those are your orders, why are you talking to *me*? I can't do anything from here," Caleb grit out.

The phone call ended.

"I said, where the fuck *are we going?*" they bit out harsher, lower, letting the anger and unfairness of the entire situation blaze through their veins.

"Oh don't try to act tough now. Haven't spilled a drop of blood, ever? Please. What are you gonna do, kiss us?" Ralph snapped from the driver's seat.

"In your fucking dreams," Xander hissed. "Just because I don't use my blade doesn't mean I don't know how. You still know how to use your dick, don't you?"

Xander silently cheered at how red his face turned.

"Speaking of, you really changed your tune quick, huh? S'all it took was some dragon dick?"

"Shut up, Ralph," Caleb snapped.

The driver's red face darkened, but he did as he was told. Finally.

It gave Xander the tiniest amount of hope, that Caleb was still defending them in *some* way. Xander let the silence lie for oh, about five seconds. "So… Destination? Where are we headed?"

Caleb groaned. "We're not telling you."

Xander snapped their gaze to him. "Why? What's going on?"

"You were compromised, man," Caleb grit out, turning to face them. His expression was pained.

Because they all knew what it meant when a hunter was compromised.

Xander's eyes widened.

"Stop the car right now," Xander demanded.

The hunter to their right, in the backseat with them twitched, their hand slowly rising to rest on the handle of the gun at their hip. Xander shook their head. "Don't do it, Ian. I've known you guys my whole fucking life," they warned.

"I know!" Caleb said from the passenger seat, frustration lacing his voice. "That's why this fucking sucks! You think it isn't hard when we lose one of our own? Especially like this?"

After Jeffrey.

Something heavy settled on Xander's chest, panic took root. "You haven't lost shit! I'm right fucking here!"

"No man, you're too far gone." Caleb was shaking his head. "You know too much about hunter operations. You can't ride the fence. There's no best of both worlds in this situation."

"Let me out of the car," Xander asked, voice dipping closer to pleading than they'd ever heard it. They'd fucking run back to Milo, even if they were already a few miles gone.

"We *can't.* Arthur's orders."

Xander's eyes fluttered shut. Arthur's orders were like law to the hunters. "Where is Arthur anyway? Why isn't he here to oversee my... my retirement."

Caleb turned around to face the windshield again. "You don't wanna know the answer to that."

The rooted panic grew, vines wrapping through their ribs and making their chest tight, carving their heart right out. Xander's heart dropped right through their feet and onto the asphalt below the car, rolling to a battered halt long behind them.

The only reason Arthur, director and fucking adoptive goddamned no good *father* would have stayed behind instead of overseeing their *retirement* would be...

"That's what plucking a scale feels like. Being skinned alive, piece by piece."

Milo's voice came back to them from that day in the forest. When Milo had traced circles into their hand and whispered the horrors that dragons faced.

"Stop the car right now." Their voice dipped, danger seeping into their words.

Xander tried to imagine a life without Milo in it, a *world* without Milo in it. Without his silly trinkets and soft clothes and his little bakery, making cakes for Patty and John, and driving his fancy car through the back roads.

This was okay when Milo could still do all that. This was *okay* when Milo was going to be alive to reap the benefits of Xander's absence.

I should've known.

Xander should've known Arthur would never let Milo live. Not after somehow, in his mind, turning his best asset against him.

"If you want to live," Xander said darkly. "You'll stop the car, right. Fucking. Now."

The driver's eyes flashed in the rear view mirror.

"Now Xander, don't be like—"

Ralph never got to finish his smarmy patronization because Xander elbowed Ian, feeling the sickening crunch of his nose beneath their bone. He cursed, one hand cupping his face and the other hand already reaching for his gun.

But Xander wrapped their zip tied hands around his wrist, slamming it against his knee again and again until his grip finally loosened with a grunt.

They snatched the gun mid-air and aimed between the front seats, firing a shot at the windshield.

The threat and promise rang in all of their ears.

The driver shouted, swerving dangerously on the road, and Caleb held a hand up as the glass cracked.

Without missing a beat, Xander pointed the gun at the back of the driver's seat.

They were all expendable. Hunters. Arthur had spent so much time preaching about family and connection and strength in solidarity. But they were no more valuable to him than a middle class worker to a CEO. They were *nothing* to him. A means to an end, *retired* at the first inconvenience.

"Turn the fucking car around," they yelled.

Silence, except for the rumble of the road beneath the tires and the breath sawing in and out of their chest, adrenaline riding them hard. Except for Ian's shaky breaths to their right, hand still cupped around his bleeding nose.

Xander's hand was unwavering around the gun, even though their chest practically rattled.

Xander had never felt rage like this. So cavernous their very soul was vibrating with it. Never before had it gone so bone deep, had their heart thumping behind their ribs with such vigor.

All because Milo needed them and they were trapped in this *fucking* car.

"Now!" they shouted, voice echoing in the closed surroundings with thinly veiled panic.

"We can't just give you the car!" Caleb hissed. "*We'll* be the ones retired if we do."

"I don't care what story you come up with to cover your asses. Just get the fuck out, leave your weapons, and let me drive away."

"Or what?" Ralph scoffed, keeping the car on the road.

"Or I'll fucking shoot you!" Xander hissed. "What part of this are you not getting?"

"First Jeffrey, now us?" Ralph spat.

"Jeffrey was… Jeffrey was an unfortunate accident," Xander whispered. "But that's the risk we take when we hunt dragons."

"There would have been *one* if you hadn't been fucking letting them go this whole time! Not two!"

"I'm *sorry!*" Xander shouted. "What we do—what the hunters do isn't *right.* It never has been. What right do we have to what's theirs?"

No one responded.

God, they were frantic with it, the need to get this car headed in the right direction, but their hand was steady as ever.

Xander was hyperaware of all three of them, each breath they took.

"Caleb, if you reach for your gun, I'm pulling the trigger. The only thing I have left to lose isn't in this car. You know I'll do it."

It didn't matter how hard they'd tried not to spill a drop of blood all these years. They'd spill *gallons* if it meant saving Milo.

And maybe he finally realized it, saw it in the crazed light in their eyes, because the driver slowed, pulling the car to a stop on the side of the road.

Ian, on their right, was the first to move, opening his car door and sliding out before slamming it shut, still holding his bloody nose and cursing as he stomped across the road.

Xander stared at the man in the passenger seat, memories flashing through their mind. Fifteen fucking years they'd spent with these people, growing trust, growing *up.*

"I love him," Xander said, if only because he was owed an explanation. "I fucking love him."

Something in Caleb's expression softened, just the smallest fraction, and he finally moved. The door cracked open and something close to relief—but still too panicked—settled in Xander's chest.

"For your sake, I hope I never see you again," he said, crooked smile softening to something sad.

Then it shifted, hardened, as he stared at the driver. "Get out, Ralph," he said, voice leaving no room for an argument. "Give them the car, and your gun."

"But how will we explain—"

Caleb's fist snapped out before Xander could register, and Ralph's head jerked to the side, followed by a curse.

"I just had my nose reset two weeks ago, you fucker," he hissed.

"Don't question me. They overpowered us and took the car. We're lucky they didn't fucking shoot us. Now get out."

His hands tightened around the wheel once, but Ralph eventually huffed and followed suit.

Caleb watched him go, looking after Xander in his own way like he had for years.

"I'm sorry," Xander said, because Caleb didn't deserve this. There would be repercussions, no matter if the HOA believed their story or not.

He removed his gun and placed it on the dashboard. "Ever since the Big Reveal, hunters are being phased out. You're lucky, getting out before it all implodes. I hope you get there in time."

They shared a sad smile that spoke volumes, and Xander would never be able to read them all in what little time they had. "Then do me a favor and get the fuck out. Or come with me."

They chalked it up to sentimentality, that the phrase left their lips.

Caleb grinned. "That's a mighty kind offer. But if you happen to kill Arthur, someone needs to be able to pick up the pieces."

"And that's you?" Xander questioned, head cocked to the side.

Xander hated the politics that came with being a hunter, but Caleb had always been oddly natural at it.

With the way they'd buried their head in the sand these past years, trying to save as many dragons as possible, Caleb had been doing his own work, they supposed.

"That's me," he said, smooth, familiar confidence sliding into place. "Sorry. You're on your own."

Xander grinned. "Not anymore."

"Stop, I'm gonna get jealous," Caleb drawled, and finally cracked open the car door. "Good luck."

"No thanks to you," they returned, falling back into their usual banter. It was easy, familiar. Made it easy to ignore the pang in their heart.

"Bye, Xander. See you never."

Ignoring the pinch of grief in their chest at the truth in his words, they nodded. "If we're lucky."

Caleb shut the door with a slam, and joined the other two on the side of the road.

In seconds, Xander was behind the wheel, throwing the car into gear, and turning the damned thing around.

They had a dragon to save.

15. A SPECIAL ANNOUNCEMENT

"This is a really nice rug," Milo wheezed, and spit a glob of blood onto the hardwood. "Please don't get my blood on it."

This Arthur guy was *pissed*, and wiped his knuckles on a handkerchief—of all things—before tucking it back into his pocket.

Milo had his escape hidden in his sleeve, but… he hadn't used it yet.

Wouldn't do him any good to go dragon and then be shot out of the sky.

He winced to himself. Fuck, what a way to go.

The plan was to get out of this alive. Somehow.

Did he have a plan?

Not in the slightest.

Actually, he was still fucking hung up on watching Xander get shoved into that SUV.

"Where'd you take Xander?" he asked, staring up at the prim, rich looking white guy. God, he was right out of a movie or something, *exactly* the kind of guy one would imagine the director of the Hunters of Obscure Artifacts.

"You have no leverage here, and therefore no right to ask any questions."

Milo took stock of the room, the two hunters by the door, the others that were probably still on his lawn. Why were they still here? Where did they take Xander?

"Do you know what happens to hunters who are compromised?" the director asked.

Milo didn't answer, because this guy—Arthur?—was going to tell him anyway. His heart sank as he pulled a pair of latex gloves from his pocket, and carefully tugged them over his fingers with the ease of practice.

"They get retired," Arthur said as he snapped the last glove on. He stalked closer, circling Milo until he was out of sight. "And as I'm sure you can imagine, that does not come with a 401K."

Milo would have rolled his eyes if it weren't for the dread sinking heavier and heavier in his gut. His hands were still bound in front of him, the key Xander slipped him now warm from resting against his skin.

He could fight, but how many hunters were there? He couldn't take them *all* on, not alone. And not when they were all armed with guns.

Why didn't Xander carry any guns? They'd unstrapped blade after blade—and even that fucking whip—had dumped it all on the entry way table as if it was nothing. But not a single gun in sight.

"So you're going to kill them? The kid you practically raised?" Milo asked, turning his head to see over his shoulder.

He spied the glint of a blade, but it never touched his skin. No, it sliced through his shirt, baring his shoulder and—

And the scales that dotted his shoulder blades, up the back of his neck.

His breath sawed in and out of his chest a little harder. Blood still welled from his split lip, but it was nothing in comparison to how bad this was about to fucking hurt.

The key now burned a hole through his sleeve, but he had to weigh his options.

Scaled alive, or risk being shot?

One was definitely going to hurt. The other... Maybe he could dodge?

His options were fucking shitty.

But... Fuck.

Maybe if he got out, he could fly off like Xander had told him to in the beginning. Maybe he could fly overhead and try to find that SUV with Xander inside. *Before* their retirement.

"Yes. I did raise Xander to be who they are today. And look how that turned out."

Milo could hear the sneer in his voice, flinching when he laid a hand against Milo's shoulder.

"How does it feel to know you're the one who killed them?"

His breath stuttered in his chest.

"Because of *you*, because of what you've done to them." The director practically spat the words. "Pliers," he snapped.

Oh, fuck this.

Milo moved slowly, urging the key out of his sleeve and cupping it in his hands.

"I didn't do anything to them. At least, nothing they didn't want." It was a cheap shot, but pissing this guy off brought him *great* joy.

Something snapped open. There was a quiet clank of metal and then a pause.

The hand returned to his shoulder, thumb and forefinger pressing in hard over his scales.

Oh fuck. Oh shit.

"If you won't tell us where your hoard is, we'll complete the mission the hard way."

"I'm not giving the hoard to anyone but Xander."

That made him pause, and Milo was smug with the

knowledge. The director had sent his only shot at retrieving the hoard to their death.

Milo felt the metal edge of the pliers nudge beneath his scale with a jolt. It sent shivers along his skin, the dread in his gut turning to nausea as he tensed in awful anticipation.

His hands were visibly shaking as he stared down at them, but he only had one shot at this.

You can sacrifice one *scale. It won't even be that bad. Right?*

His pep talk did *nothing* to abate the dread, but he needed the director distracted. Needing him looking somewhere other than at Milo's hands.

Like watching a scale being ripped out of his skin.

"I'm going to enjoy this, so please don't be quiet for my sake."

If Milo wasn't freaking the *fuck* out, he would've snapped back with something witty, maybe even something crass. Instead he was sweating in the chair, hands shaking.

The pliers closed hard around his scale and for a split second Milo was rocked silent from the pain. He *heard* the snap of the edge of the scale lift away from his skin, felt the blood well and begin to drip down his back. He bit his lip so hard he drew blood from the fresh cut, but it was nothing compared to the searing pain at his back.

The director was cruel with it, instead of ripping it off like a band-aid, he was taking his sweet time, pulling just hard enough to rip the scale out a millimeter at a time.

Breathing past the pain—barely—Milo dug the key into the old lock of the cuffs. To disguise the sound, he jolted and let fly the loud, vehement curse he'd trapped behind his teeth. It echoed around the room.

He could sense the fucker's depraved smile. Wondered how Xander ever let this man fool them into thinking he was… what? A father figure?

How fucked up was Xander's childhood that *this* man was their best option?

The hole in his skin throbbed as the scale was finally yanked free. Milo felt his heartbeat in each pulse, the blood welling up and dripping anew with each beat of his heart.

God, it fucking *burned*, his eyes stung with it.

"Well, there's one," Arthur drawled.

Milo tensed as he felt the pliers bite around another scale, and he shook his head. Hell no was this bastard taking another one.

"Have something to say suddenly?"

Milo waited until the pliers pulled away before he let the cuffs drop, and scales flowed down his arms, talons extended his nails. He turned in the chair in an instant, barely noting the surprise on Arthur's face before Milo's arm snapped out, fist colliding with his nose.

The two hunters from the door turned at the commotion, and Milo dove behind the couch before their gunfire littered the cushions.

His shoulder still throbbed, but the adrenaline must have been doing its best work. He was able to ignore it as he waited for the gunfire to pause. When it did, he pushed the scales out to cover the rest of his body before he dove for the window.

It burst around him, but the scales protected his skin as he rolled and shifted onto the grass.

Commotion was already stirring around the house, shouts and curses littering the air.

If Milo flew away, he wouldn't be able to defend himself.

Tail flicking behind him, he huffed out a hot breath and waited. He hated breathing fire, and he really liked his green lawn; it looked so nice but, fuck it.

Rounding the corner of the house, Milo began to build

the heat in his throat, but the rev of an engine cut through the night and his heat sputtered as dread filled him.

There was.

But not their backup.

His.

A very fucking familiar face squinted through a cracked windshield, expression alarmed and furious as the SUV skidded to a halt.

The hunters were torn, some taking aim at the vehicle, and some lifting their weapons toward him. They were unorganized, panicking.

Milo growled, charging forward at the hunters.

Shots flew through the air, but thankfully his scales reflected the ones that hit, and he swung his tail around, taking out a whole row of them. They yelled as they were tossed across the lawn, sent rolling down the very hill Milo had protected Xander from only days ago.

As expected, he drew the attention of the majority of them, orders ringing out from some of them as they yelled to each other to redirect.

Milo just wanted to get himself between the hunters and Xander.

Xander, who—did they have a *gun?*

He watched them take aim, and with a flash of light and a *bang,* one of the hunters went down, shouting and holding his shoulder.

Oh, so we're not *killing them?*

Milo, personally, had some thoughts about that, but he could wait and share later. He had more pressing matters to attend to.

Dragons were huge, okay? They made a big target, so it wasn't a surprise when one of the men actually aimed for a soft spot, and hit.

Pain bloomed bright and red from his flank, on the inside of his leg where his scales grew sparse.

He roared, the sound alone enough to scare some of the men into pausing, eyes wide and frozen in fear. Milo didn't stop them as they broke away from the fight to climb into another black vehicle. They peeled out with a screech of tires, but Xander lifted their gun and aimed, firing off two shots that took out one of the tires just as they reached the road.

Milo snapped his arm out, claws withdrawn, and gathered up a group of three men. They shouted and wiggled, but before they could clench their fingers around the triggers, he threw them at the remaining group. Very Godzilla style, he couldn't help but think with a huff of a chuckle.

They went down in a pile, a few shots fired in the panic, the scent of copper filling the air.

Milo shifted when he grew close enough to Xander and rolled into his human form behind the vehicle they'd arrived in. It was the only thing standing between them and the pile of hunters.

"Hi," Milo said, chest heaving and winced at the pain in his shoulder.

The wound in his leg was taken care of as he shifted. Don't ask him how it worked, he didn't fucking know, he was just grateful. But scales were a different story. They didn't regrow with the magic of the shift, because they were missing in both dragon and human forms.

"Hi," Xander whispered, expression soft with relief and worry.

"Personally, so glad you've arrived," Milo said, a tense smile curling his lips. "But on a scale of one to fucked, now what?"

Xander frowned at his ripped shirt, and gripped the uninjured shoulder to pull him away from the door of the vehicle.

They leaned over him to look at his back and cursed before releasing him abruptly. "Bastard. I'll kill them, that's what," they practically growled before leaning into the open door of the SUV and pulling out two more weapons. "I'm so sorry, Milo, I got here as fast as I could."

"Weren't you like, on your way to an execution or something? Oh, I really don't like guns," Milo said, but let Xander hand him one anyway.

"Yes, and now I'm not. If you prefer going all dragon, that's fine too."

"I do prefer that to be honest," he admitted, and passed it back to them.

"Great," Xander drawled, and tucked it in the waistband of their pants before standing up and peering over the hood of the car. They narrowed their eyes before lowering back to his level. "I'm *really* glad you're okay."

Their voice was rough with emotion, but before Milo could get a handle on the way his heart skipped, they stood and held out a hand to him.

Milo stared at the slim shape of their fingers, the lines of their palm. And suddenly, Milo couldn't help but imagine that night in the alley, days ago. When Xander had first cuffed them together and their roles were reversed as Milo had stood, offering them his hand. At the time, they'd slapped his hand away in a huff of annoyance and stubbornness.

But now Milo slid his hand into theirs, let them heft him to his feet with a grunt. Their touch lingered for only a second before their expression hardened and they walked around the vehicle.

"Oh, you meant, like *now*," Milo said, and let his magic wash over him. He was bigger than the car by *far* as a dragon, so it didn't offer much protection anyway, and he followed Xander, letting them lead.

The hunters were still scattered across the lawn, moaning and groaning and—

The one closest to them sat up, gun outstretched in his hand, but before he could even think about pulling the trigger, Xander's gun went off and the man jerked back, blood welling in his shoulder as he shouted.

Milo huffed, the warm breath fluttering Xander's dark hair.

Competency was so hot on them.

God, adrenaline was *such* a rush. Or maybe it was the relief that Xander was okay.

The missing scale still burned, still ached and throbbed with each beat of his heart, but it was easier to ignore when he was a dragon.

The front door opened, and the director reappeared, expression sullen once again.

"Xander what are you *doing?*" he yelled, voice carrying across the lawn.

The hunters who were quickly recovering and untangling themselves froze, gazes darting between the two as Arthur stomped off the porch, waving for the hunters to stand down. Xander's fingers resettled on the weapon, but they didn't lift it, even as he drew closer.

"Coming out of retirement early," Xander said, voice hard.

A hunter to their right groaned and tried to lift his gun, but Milo lifted a clawed foot and brought it down over his arm. He cursed and tried to tug his arm free, but Milo leaned harder until he groaned and gave up.

"You're fighting *us*? Your fam—"

"Oh, shut the fuck up about family!" Xander yelled, taking a step forward. Milo was floored by the sheer, thinly veiled emotion in their cracked voice. "You were going to have me killed! And you weren't even going to be there!"

"Well, I'm here now," he said, though his voice was far from comforting, low and dangerous. "Kill them!" he shouted the demand, waiting for the hunters to leap into action.

Instinctively, Milo curled his tail around the front of Xander, halting their path and tugging them back against him. He knew it was their fight, but he didn't trust this bastard in the least.

"You're on a fucking power trip—"

A bright flash interrupted, softening to a glow, golden in its brilliance and filling the lawn so bright Milo had to look away. When it faded, Milo shifted back to his half human form, eyes bugging right out of his head.

"Oh, is this a bad time?" the demon asked, taking in the spilled hunters and the tense standoff.

"What do *you* want?" Milo asked, dread curdling his stomach once again. He vaguely recognized the demon, but couldn't remember his name.

"I have a summons from Lucifer for the dragons," he said. "I'm Julian, seventh messenger of the seventh region of Hell. Do you have a moment to talk about our lord and savior?"

The pause was painfully tense before Julian broke out in a grin. "Sorry, I've always wanted to say that. Never had the opportunity until now."

"I'm sorry—Lucifer?" Arthur practically yelled, salt and peppered hair a mess across his forehead, face red from his vehemence.

Julian arched a brow. "The one and only. Should I care who you are?"

Arthur swallowed, taking a step back from the demon, and Milo chuckled. "You know dragons and all the other creatures exist, but you didn't pause to wonder about Hell?"

Julian's wings shuffled. "If you want these men to live, you better tell the one behind me to lower his goddamned weapon," he growled, wings twitching in irritation.

Arthur blinked, before cutting his hand through the air. "Stand down!" he shouted.

Xander leaned closer to Milo during this exchange, and he absorbed their warmth with something akin to glee. "Do you know what's going on?" they asked.

"Remember how I told you we're from Hell?" He waited for Xander to nod before he continued. "I guess Lucifer figured out we're gone," he answered, before stepping forward.

His mind raced with possibilities. Was Lucifer pissed and demanding their return? Was he waiting to punish them? What the fuck was going on? Why *now*?

"You said you had a summons?"

"Yes, exactly." Julian unfurled an ancient looking scroll and frowned at the words before humming. "Hold on now. This isn't a summons at all. It's just a message..."

"From *Lucifer*?" Milo hissed, sharing a wide eyed look with Xander.

"Yes. Apparently I'm supposed to read it to you." Julian did not sound happy about this development, eyes glazing over as he read ahead through the document. "Yeah, I'm not reading all this. It basically says..."

Xander and Milo both leaned forward.

"He's not upset that you left Hell with no word, and at this time he doesn't request your presence. He does, however, take offense that you've all disa-*fucking*-ppeared." Julian's eyes lifted to them. "Yes, that was his exact word. Anyway, blah blah *oh!* This is good—"

Milo refrained from snatching the scroll himself so he could get to the point.

"He's pissed that Milo is the first dragon who's actually where he's supposed to be—you have no idea how many locations I've visited in the past week. A *lot* of you have died or are missing in action—and he wants to know if it's because of the HOA. Hmm…" Julian's brows furrowed. "Yeah he rambles about that for a bit, not a happy camper there." The demon lifts his gaze to Arthur, who's eyes were wide, trying to look innocent. "Lucifer offers the full support of his army if the hunters are a problem. Aw… Luci is getting soft—*don't tell him I said that*—he even says he's sorry he hasn't noticed until now. Doesn't say why though. Damn."

"Is there a point to this?" Milo asked in a huff. "Lucifer sent you all the way here to tell us that he's *not* mad at the dragons for getting the hell out of dodge?"

"Yes. And to offer assistance with wiping out the hunters, if necessary," he said, finally folding the scroll and clasping his hands in front of him. His golden wings twitched.

Xander cleared their throat, and the demon's attention shifted. "I don't think the hunters are going to be a problem anymore." They aimed a pointed look towards Arthur, who's lips thinned out of anger.

"We're just gonna take his word for it?" Milo asked. "That just doesn't seem like the smartest plan." He didn't trust Arthur one bit, and neither should Xander.

"Oh, this guy? The director, I suppose?" Julian suggested pointedly, glaring at Arthur. He sized him up, humming to himself before he nodded. "Yes. I think he'll come with me."

Arthur backed up, eyes wide. "Now, hold on."

"Unless your little hunters have an objection? Wait, let me read you something first." Julian announced, a smug grin curling his lips. He unfolded the scroll again and Milo rolled his eyes.

Fucking demons and their fancy scrolls and golden wings. For fuck's sake.

"If the hunters do not cooperate with this new law and order, the dragons have the full support of the Hellish army, capital H, laws of the new world be damned." Julian lowered the scroll. "The consequences will be swift and unimaginably severe, as I'm sure you understand." The demon spoke directly to the hunters still clambering to their feet, eyes wide and unsure as they shared glances with one another.

"So. Any objections?"

Not a single hunter spoke up, and Milo blinked at the pressure he felt wrap around his hand. He squeezed Xander back.

"Milo, give me your phone," Julian demanded.

Milo jolted, wondering if the softness suddenly filling his chest was apparent on his face.

He pulled the phone from his pocket—don't ask him how it survived the shifting either, he didn't know—and handed it over. The demon's prim fingers glided over the screen until he hummed in satisfaction. "Lucifer will be in touch."

"With me?" Milo squeaked, and then cleared his throat. "Why?"

"Because you've got to get all the dragons to come out of hiding. Was that not clear?"

Milo's eye twitched. "No, that wasn't clear. Was this in the scroll?"

"Oh, did I leave that out?"

Xander mumbled something along the lines of "what a fucking messenger".

"Uh, yes. Care to elaborate?" Milo answered diplomatically.

Julian's eyes twinkled. "No, I don't think I will. Good luck!"

Before Milo could even part his lips to argue, Julian disappeared.

"Fuuuck," Milo groaned, turning to Xander, but their gaze was locked across the lawn, at the director, Arthur. He was slinking away, and Xander took a step forward, but before they could do anything at all Julian reappeared in a flash of gold light.

"Sorry, forgot something," he said sheepishly. He clapped his hands, and Arthur disappeared with him. For good, this time.

Hopefully.

In place of Julian, Milo could now see the hunters staring wide eyed at one another.

"Now what?" Milo murmured to Xander.

Hunters were their people, and it seemed no matter what, the hunters recognized this too, staring at Xander as if waiting for their next orders.

They huffed. "What are you staring at me for? Get the fuck outta here!"

As they retreated to their vehicles, the sound of an engine nearing grew louder, echoing off Milo's house and the trees, until a Honda Accord's tires crackled over the driveway.

"Oh shit," Xander breathed, and stepped closer to Milo, actually stepping in front of him. Which, if Milo wasn't so turned on right then, he would've probably protested.

The hunter who'd taken Xander away peeled himself out of the sedan and took in the scene with narrowed eyes.

"Where's Arthur?"

16. LEATHER TOUCH

"Where's Arthur?"

Just at the sound of his name, their chest ached with equal parts grief and anger. They glanced over their shoulder at Milo, unsure of how much they were allowed to share. "Can I tell him?"

"I mean, it's not so secret anymore, is it?" Milo asked, waving a hand at the hunters still moving too slowly for their liking.

More than one of them looked at Caleb in relief, and Xander suddenly pieced together the haphazard puzzle.

Caleb's uncanny ease with politics. The phone call from the car. *I can't do anything from here.*

How long had he been usurping Arthur's control of the hunters?

Xander stepped forward with something like relief blooming in their chest, ignored Ralph and Ian as they crawled from the sedan and went to talk to the other hunters.

"I don't wanna fight demons," one of them said, voice carrying in a hiss across the landscape. "Can they *teleport?* That's badass."

Xander almost laughed.

"Arthur's gone," Xander said, watching every nuance of Caleb's expression.

It didn't even shift. Impressive.

"Hell is real," they continued, and this time Caleb's eyebrow twitched. Xander tried not to smile. "God, you're so good at that," they groaned. "Fucker."

Caleb's lips finally twisted into a small smile, and he flicked his gaze to the hunters, all on standby, murmurs filling the air.

"I thought I wasn't supposed to see you again," Caleb said calmly.

"You're the one that drove here. Who's car is that?"

The hunter shrugged. "Some poor guy. He's in the trunk. *Not* dead, before you ask. I'm not heartless."

"Could've fooled me," Xander said dryly. "Anyway, a demon from Hell came, had a big fancy scroll and every-thing. Threatened to offer the dragons the full force of the… Milo, what'd he say?" they asked, turning to find their dragon.

Milo stepped forward at the sound of his name, glaring at Caleb as he answered. His protectiveness made their heart thump against their chest. "Dragons have the full support of the Hellish army, capital H, laws of the new world be damned were his exact words, I believe."

"Wow, you really were Hell's messengers. Poor Julian, having to live up to your name," Xander teased before turning back to Caleb. "Then he took Arthur with him. Apparently Lucifer is upset that the dragons are displaced and missing. Blames the hunters."

Caleb's brow was so furrowed Xander wondered if he would ever be able to unknit it. "Well, this certainly is a… ah… development."

"Kinda works in your favor if you ask me," Milo said, and Xander nodded in agreement.

"Julian didn't seem too happy," Xander mused.

"Oh, he's always like that," Milo murmured softly. "Kinda bitchy."

Xander startled at the laugh that boomed out of Caleb. He clapped Xander on the shoulder, eyes twinkling.

"I think you're right. This *does* work in our favor. Of course, I'm not going to tell you how, seeing as you're *retired*," Caleb said with a forced hint.

Xander's eyes widened, hand reaching over to Milo without a second thought, hope filling their chest until they felt bubbly. Like a glass of champagne or something else fancy.

"Oh," was all they could come up with.

Caleb's lips twitched, and Milo coughed a laugh into his shoulder. They'd get him back for that. Later.

Because apparently that was a thing now.

Later. With Milo.

They barely managed to corral their expression into something neutral, instead of the utter giddiness fizzing through their system.

"Well," Xander dragged out the word before offering Caleb their hand. "Good luck with the hunters."

"We're gonna have to rebrand," Caleb said, and clasped Xander's hand in his own. They shook briefly before releasing. "Enjoy retirement."

"I will," Xander replied softly, fighting the urge to turn their head to look at Milo. They wanted the hunters gone first.

"Now, get them off my lawn," Milo growled, nodding his head toward the hunters awaiting orders.

Caleb smiled tightly. "Well, you heard the dragon. Get outta here," he called, waving his hand at the group. "I'll see you all at HQ. Keep your mouth shut about this until I can make an announcement."

They grumbled slightly, but it was only a handful of moments before it was just Xander and Milo, the quiet of the night, and the mess of the lawn. Tire tracks marred the manicured grass, the front door was still hanging open, and —was that a broken window?

Xander finally turned to face Milo, the moon bright overhead and casting him in a soft glow. "Hi," they said, lamely.

"Hi yourself," Milo murmured.

"Can I take you up on that tea now?" Xander asked.

They weren't quite ready to process the events of the last few hours. The way their entire life had changed in such a short time.

"How about a soft robe to go with it?" he offered.

Xander nodded, cheeks flushing as the words Milo had uttered to them last night fluttered through their head.

Nothing felt real as they crossed the lawn, as Milo held the door for them. To the right, through the parlor doors, they spied the aftermath. The pretty velvet couch was littered with bullet holes, the window right behind it shattered.

Xander had done this too, even if indirectly.

"Maybe a shower first," they rasped, voice suddenly raw, throat tight with unshed tears. They wanted to wash the night off. They didn't... They couldn't...

"Hey," Milo said softly, fingers threading through their own and pulling them around to face him. "This was... a lot, yeah?"

Xander nodded.

Milo shut the parlor doors, locking them tight before leading Xander down the hallway. Through his bedroom to the huge bathroom, cranking the steamy water on. As he did so, he turned his back to Xander, revealing the bloody space where his scale had been.

They must have made a sound in their throat, because

Milo whirled around, eyes wide. He rushed to Xander, who wrapped their arms around his waist, squeezing tight.

"I'm sorry," they whispered into his chest. "I'm so sorry."

"You don't have *anything* to be sorry for," Milo said. He tried to keep his voice level, but it hardened as he palmed Xander's shoulders and pushed them back. "Do you understand what you did?"

Xander nodded. "I put you in dange—"

"No," Milo growled, and the force of his tone made Xander's eyes go wide. "You... you *chose* me. In front of all those hunters. Over your family. Even your... your dad, Xander."

Now Milo's voice was the one tight in his throat, and Xander's eyes welled with tears. "Family wouldn't ask that of me. I couldn't do it. I *wouldn't*."

Milo palmed the back of their head and pulled them in tight. His throat clicked as he swallowed. "I know. I know."

"It's all my fault," Xander confessed. "The reason they showed up. They found out what I've been doing. One of the dragons I helped was with a dragon they were targeting. When the hunter arrived, they overpowered him because he was only expecting one dragon. Not two. So they came here to... to—"

"Retaliate. Get answers. Accuse you."

Those were all as good as any word that currently escaped Xander's grasp. They nodded, cheek pressing against Milo.

"I left you here," they murmured.

Milo made a dubious noise in his throat. "You came back."

"And they—he hurt you," Xander said, voice small.

"But only so much as I let him," Milo said, squeezing Xander tight. "I let it distract him while I used the key. The key *you* somehow stole and slipped me, even under the eye of all those hunters. Fuck, Xander, you really have no idea how fucking unreal you are."

They ran their hands over his back, over the shirt but afraid to let their touch drift higher. "Can I take care of you?" Xander asked.

Milo pulled back, brow furrowed. "But that's my job."

"Just this once," they promised, refusing to take no for an answer. "Do you have a first aid kit?"

After shutting the water off, Milo sat on the bed while Xander knelt behind him, dabbing at the circular wound of his missing scale. The pile of cotton balls were stained red, but Xander kept their motions light and gentle, tuned into Milo's every flinch and muffled hiss.

"Why don't these heal like your bullet wound did?"

"'Cause it's a scale. It's different somehow, though I don't know the science or magic or whatever behind it."

"Oh," they said coherently. "Well, that's stupid."

Milo chuckled, shoulders shaking as he laughed, and Xander paused their dabbing to glare at the wound. It was clean, if bright red from irritation. They packed it with gauze and bandaged him up, fingers quick and deft from practice as they taped it down.

"Don't get it wet for a while."

The sound that came out of Milo was something close to a whine. "But then how am I going to shower with you?"

Xander's grin made their cheeks hurt, and they pressed a kiss to the very edge of his shoulder. "Very carefully?"

They were too proud to admit that Milo pulled a gasp out of them as he turned suddenly, scooping Xander up. They wrapped their legs around him, and held onto the undamaged shoulder as Milo stalked them to the bathroom. "I'll show you carefully," he murmured.

"But your shoulder," Xander said in their best chastising voice.

"Oh, it'll be sore for a while. But if you think that's gonna stop me from having you every which way to Sunday, you're so wrong."

Xander's lips twitched. "How wrong?"

"The most wrong."

"And you're gonna set me right, are you?"

"Maybe."

Milo sat them on the counter, and pressed in close, sidling himself between their legs. Xander trailed their hands down his chest, fingers catching the flap of the ripped shirt and rubbing it between their fingertips.

"I liked this shirt on you," Xander whispered.

With a chuckle, Milo stripped the rest of it off. "I'll get another one, if you like."

They couldn't help the twitch of their lips. "Yeah, yeah."

Milo covered their hand with one of his own, the leather of their gloves warming under his touch. Slowly, carefully, more carefully than they deserved, he held their hand out between them, fingers tracing their palm through the leather.

The playfulness to the moment dissolved into something warmer, something heavy.

"The first time I saw you, I almost couldn't be convinced you were real. All hot and mysterious by the bar. These fucking gloves."

Xanders heart sped up as he drifted his touch to their left wrist, where the glove ended. He slid a finger beneath the hem of the glove at the heel of their palm.

Their breath caught at just the innocent touch, watching as Milo inched up the buttery fabric bit by bit.

"I'd like to say something romantic, like this is the last time you'll ever have to take these off, but... that would be *such* a tragedy."

Xander's lips twitched. "They do kinda help with gripping your scales in flight."

His eyes actually brightened at Xander's words as he gazed up at them. "Yeah! Well, that's great then. Yep."

Xander smirked as he cleared his throat and traced the intricate stitching from beneath. The knuckle of his finger brushed against their palm. Slowly, reverently, he lifted their hand to his lips. He pressed a gentle kiss to their fingertips, and Xander's smile turned soft.

Oh, but *then*, Milo took their middle finger between his lips to the first knuckle, into the hot cavern of his mouth. Then the second, until his teeth closed around the base of their finger, over the leather of the glove. He bit, caught the leather behind his teeth, and pulled, tugging the glove as he retreated.

As Xander's mind blanked with arousal, Milo kissed their palm when it was bare, and the glove landed on the tiled floor with a soft *plop*.

"You know, when I asked you if I could take care of you..." Xander began, and removed their palm from Milo's grasp.

Their smile almost returned at the sight of his disappointment.

He wouldn't be disappointed for long.

Xander lifted their gloved hand and dragged it from the front of his shoulder down his chest, lower, to his happy scales—affectionately, officially forevermore named that—and stopped at his waistband.

Interest darkened his gaze, and Xander's lips quirked up at him.

"I meant in every way."

Milo swallowed. "W-with the glove?" he choked out.

"With the glove," Xander agreed, because Milo was down bad for it, and they... they just wanted to kiss him about it.

Xander took advantage of the height they had from the counter, and wrapped their ungloved hand around Milo's neck to pull him forward. A chaste, sweet kiss at first, but they licked at his lips for more. He opened for them in the sweetest way.

Their bare hand traced the shape of the smaller scales at the back of his neck, and when his hips inched forward into their palm, they grinned into the kiss. In a few less than suave attempts, they got his pants open—it was a little difficult with one hand, alright?—and slipped their palm beneath the waistband.

Milo gasped into the kiss as they wrapped their leather clad palm around him. He was hot to the touch, even through the glove, as his hips kicked into their fist.

"Already so wet for me," Xander breathed, more than a little feverish with the knowledge. Stroking him from root to tip, they tightened their grip on the upstroke, encouraging more precum to spill generously over their fingers.

Milo wrapped his hands around their waist, something to hold onto, as he nodded into the kiss.

"How does it feel? With the leather?" they asked softly, tilting their head back to catch a glimpse of their dragon.

His eyes were closed, face screwed up and jaw slack with pleasure. He nodded, but didn't answer, and Xander arched a brow before they stopped the steady movements of their hand.

A soft groan spilled past his lips at that, his eyes drifting open in confusion.

"How does it feel?" they asked again.

His gaze darkened, hips twitching into their fist, and they loosened their grip so he had nothing to rut against.

The groan he let loose was deeper this time, more desperate as he nodded. "It's perfect," he said quickly. "Hot and good and don't *stop* for fuck's sake," he whined.

It took every bit of self control not to smile. Milo wore desperation as finely as his silk shirts.

They resumed their strokes, watching his expression shutter once again as they tightened their fist. He was slick against their bare fingers and the slide was easy and... and *fuck.*

Xander glanced between them, the head of Milo's cock shadowing into their leather-clad palm again and again.

Milo was clearly onto something here.

"Look," they whispered, and Milo dropped his head down. Another groan spilled out in the same way he spilled slick over their fist, and Xander chuckled as they slid their grip lower, cupping and gently rolling his balls in their hand.

They locked their gaze on his expression as they teased a finger over the sensitive spot just below. His hips canted forward, and they wrapped their fingers around his length again, questions and visions filling their mind and making the heat between their legs flare.

With purposeful strokes, they worked him closer to the edge, basking in his harsh breaths and hushed moans and—

They tilted his head up, licked into his mouth and tasted the pleasure right from his lips.

They waited until he was tensing beneath their hands, hips urging faster and breath catching before they slowed their strokes. He groaned, and pulled back, half-lidded gaze furrowed in horny frustration.

"Why are you so mean to me?" he asked.

Xander bit down on their smile. "I was just wondering..."

He perked up at that. "What?"

Once again, they slid their touch lower, and he jolted at the gentle touch behind his balls.

"Have you ever... with a man? Or anyone else?"

His gaze darkened and he slid a hand up from their waist to the side of their neck, tilting their head at him, as if Xander's gaze was anywhere else than on the dragon at their mercy.

He began to talk as Xander drifted their touch back to his cock, squeezed once before resuming their strokes. His eyes fluttered shut but he forced them back open.

"I've been around for a few centuries. At this point." He swallowed, and Xander watched the concentration threaten to slip from his grasp. "At this point, I think it'd be a little weird if I—ah, if I hadn't."

"Would you let… me?" Xander asked softly.

Milo groaned, and his hands tightened, tugging them to the edge of the counter.

"Would you let me fuck you?" they asked, squeezing their fist around the tip of him, delighting in the slick that spilled over their fingers.

"*Fuck*, Xander," he groaned from deep in his chest, hips grinding into each stroke.

They quickened the pace, suddenly desperate to see Milo come apart beneath their touch, if only so they could put him back together. To know that he trusted them.

"Granted," they whispered, "we'd have to pick out what you wanted to be fucked with."

Milo's hips stuttered, and a second later he was stiffening, a soft, heartfelt groan echoing around the bathroom. Xander stroked him through it, the fever in them burning as he pulsed in their grip and came over their fist and panted into a messy, perfect kiss.

"So… I'll take that as a yes?" they teased breathlessly.

Milo chuckled, cheeks flushed and red and *fuck, what a sight* he made, all fucked out like that just from Xander.

He made quick work of stepping out of his pants and shoes before he cranked the shower on. Then he helped Xander out of their clothes, ignoring the wet *plop* of the second glove.

He tugged them into the spray, shoving them under the hot water.

"That was *definitely* a yes. Fuck, Xander."

Milo kissed and nipped and teased at their neck, their jaw, and attempted to go lower. In a panic, Xander fisted his hair at the base of his neck and tugged him back up.

They did *not* expect the soft moan that escaped.

"Sorry," Xander breathed. "Don't... uh, don't get your shoulder wet."

Milo surged forward, cupped a wet hand to the back of their neck and tilted them up for a kiss. It was wet and a little uncoordinated in their excitement, but that made it all the more affectionate.

"I love you," Milo murmured once he pulled back, and Xander's chest went fizzy as their mind filled with white noise.

Milo blinked, pulled back, and laughed. "Uh, I mean, in a totally casual, normal way. Y'know, as, I mean—"

"I love you too," Xander admitted. "Uh, I mean, in a really cool, practically bro-like way—"

"Shut *up*," Milo groaned, and tasted the laugh right off their lips.

"Casual," Xander mused, mid-kiss.

"I panicked, okay?" Milo groused. "You shoulda seen the look on your face."

"My face?" Xander asked, all indignant-like. "What about you?"

"You expressed an emotion, I'm allowed to be a little shocked."

"I express emotion plenty," Xander argued.

Milo leveled them with a stare, and Xander slowly accepted defeat. "I guess emotions haven't always been my strong suit."

"And what is your strong suit?"

"Take a guess."

"Combat? Weaponry?" he guessed, words spoken into

Xander's neck. He lifted his head suddenly. "You looked so hot with a gun, by the way. Your aim was impressive."

Xander shrugged, determined not to let the flush color their cheeks. Probably failed. "I told you, shooting range on Mondays."

Milo snorted, shaking his head. "I should've seen that coming."

17. BUBBLIES

For once, Xander woke up without a threat over their head, a clock ticking down.

They did awake with a cold pillow beneath their cheek, which wasn't their newfound favorite place to be. They frowned, drifting a hand across the sheets and finding more chilly bed absent of their dragon.

Blearily, they cracked their eyes open and found the bed indeed empty. They almost, *almost* let worry rattle around their head before they heard the clink and clatter of noise from the kitchen.

A smile already twitched at their lips as they eased from the bed, pulled on a robe from the chest at the end of the bed, and padded down the hallway to the kitchen.

Milo was turned toward the stove, domestic as fuck as he fried something in a pan.

Quietly, they slid onto one of the bar chairs and waited patiently for Milo to notice them. He was humming to himself, competing with the sizzle of bacon in the pan. The mess of the counter made Xander think pancakes, and they bided their time, watching as Milo scooped a spatula under a pale round circle in the pan and lifted it before they spoke.

"Good morning."

"Jesus!" Milo shouted, spatula going haywire in his hand and sending the pancake sailing through the air. It landed on the floor with a splat, and Xander covered their mouth to hide their grin as Milo spun to face them. "You *wraith*," he hissed.

They stared at the dead pancake with amusement.

"Well, that one's yours," Milo drawled.

Xander teased Milo the entire morning, watching him in blissful domesticity, and letting themself enjoy it. They'd never had something like this, someone who wanted to take care of them, someone who wanted to be with them for no reason other than because they enjoyed being around Xander.

Milo had said *I love you.*

Fighting an infectious grin, Xander kicked the chair next to them out as Milo approached, plates in hand.

"So I was thinking about finding the dragons… starting tomorrow," Milo said softly, staring at them while Xander ate their first bite.

The pancake was perfect and fluffy and buttery. They let a more than indulgent groan leave their lips just to see Milo's eyes both light up with pride *and* darken with want.

But their chest went tight at his words and they swallowed against it.

"Tomorrow? That's so soon," they responded once they let the information sink in, keeping their voice level.

Milo nodded. "Yeah, when Lucifer tells you to do something, you don't exactly take your time with it."

Mind still spinning with the knowledge that Lucifer himself existed, Xander nodded briskly. "Yep, makes sense."

"So, with that in mind, what are you doing tonight?" he asked.

Xander cut their gaze in his direction. "I don't know, let me check my schedule," they drawled.

Now that they were out of the life, they didn't exactly have a whole lot *to* do.

Milo's lips twitched and despite the worry threatening to take hold, Xander had half a mind to kiss it off him. "Good. It's a date, then."

Something fizzy and bright burst to life in Xander's chest, and they swallowed it down alongside a sip of coffee in between bites. "Alright," Xander tried to say casually. Probably didn't succeed though, because—holy shit. A date. With Milo.

Before Milo potentially left. To go find the dragons *Xander* had a hand in displacing.

"Don't worry, I'll let you borrow something," he announced with a wink. "Maybe that velvet shirt you tried on the other night."

Xander arched a brow. "You mean it survived? You ripped it off me rather... aggressively."

His cheeks flushed as he shook his head. "If that one didn't survive, I have more."

"I think you have a shopping addiction," Xander teased.

"Oh please, like it matters?" Milo said defensively. "I'll turn you into a shopping addict too."

"Why, are you gonna be my sugar dragon?"

Milo choked on his bite and had to cough, and Xander patted him on the back, avoiding the hurt shoulder with another guilty pang in their chest.

"What kind of benefits do I get with this?"

"Hmm. Well, you get to see me in all the things you buy," Xander offered. He *definitely* could afford it, but they refrained from asking about the hoard. Maybe Milo would tell them one day, but they were surprised to find they didn't care.

Of course they were curious, and it was fun to imagine.

Milo was so... extra. Did he have a secret passageway? A hidden room? What if he buried it somewhere?

What if there really was a map with an X that marked the spot?

They grinned privately, finishing off their breakfast. Maybe they could track it down together one day. Maybe even as a date.

Xander liked the idea of more dates with Milo.

They couldn't help but imagine all the places they'd visit together, all the things Xander would get to experience alongside Milo.

You know... *if* he took them with him on his dragon-finding journey.

God, were they fucking crazy or what? They'd known this dragon all of a handful of days and they were absolutely *giddy* over the thought of traveling the world with him?

Xander glanced over at Milo, watched him slam pancake after pancake back, and chuckled. He paused, a corner of a pancake hanging from his mouth like a... like a *dragon* as he glanced at them as if caught in headlights.

Their dragon.

"What?" he asked around his bite.

"Nothing," Xander said fondly.

Standing quickly, before they did something embarrassing like admit how obsessed they were, Xander gathered their plate and took it to the sink, rinsing the syrup off before sticking it in the dishwasher. They cleaned up after Milo, humor bubbling over at the absolute *mess* covering the kitchen counter.

If Milo cooked like this all the time, Xander didn't mind cleaning up after him in this relationship.

They paused, a dish halfway in the dishwasher as the thought crossed their mind.

Relationship.

It seemed a little presumptuous, but they laid the plate in the rack with a shug.

"So I *did* order something for you this morning," Milo said softly, bringing his plate closer.

Xander paused, shut the water off, and turned to him. "What is it?"

Milo cleared his throat. "You can tell me to fuck right off. I just know it got damaged literally the first night we met and I still feel kinda bad about that whole thing, what with losing the key in the lake and all. Not that I regret it, of course, because I mean, look, we made it out the other side of it all, right? Together. And that's kinda cool—"

"Milo," Xander interrupted, fighting the smile trying to curl their lips. "What did you order for me?"

"A new jacket," he blurted. "I used the tag off the one you were wearing and ordered it from their website. I just figure if you're gonna be around—"

Xander was totally, irrevocably gone for this silly, sweet, pretty dragon.

"And I'm gonna be around, am I?"

"W-well, I hoped so," Milo said, cheeks flushing.

Xander slid a hand on either side of his hips against the counter, held his gaze that was dark with worry. "I could tell you were attached to it, and you looked rather dangerously sexy in it, if I do say so myself. I just want you to be comfortable here— Wherever you are. You don't *have* to be here. No one can tell you what to do, but what I'm saying is I hope you *will* be here—"

Their chest was almost too full to take a breath. "Milo, thank you," Xander interrupted, letting the chuckle burst past their lips. They leaned in and placed a chaste, quick kiss on his slack lips. "That was really thoughtful of you." Another kiss. "I appreciate it." One more for good luck. "And yes, I will be *here*." They arched a brow. "I assume that's alright with you."

"Alright. Yep," he said, gaze flicking from Xander's lips back to their eyes again. "Here."

"Good," they said simply, and kissed him once more, syrup sweetness overwhelming their senses. Xander squeezed his hips before going back to rinsing the dishes.

It was true they hadn't had a chance to exactly peruse the internet for a replacement. Milo just saved them the trouble.

Milo blinked over at them for a long, drawn out second before he seemed to process the past few moments, and crossed his arms, watching Xander. "You're cute when you're domestic," Milo teased.

"Cute? Ew." Xander shuddered playfully. "Hate that for me."

"I don't," Milo said, wrapping his arms around their waist once they were done. "Dangerous, impressive, scary, hot. And cute."

He tucked his head into their neck and Xander leaned back into him.

"God, we *are* so fucking domestic," Xander whined, catching their reflection in the windowpane.

"It's kinda hot," Milo mused, chest bouncing with barely contained laughter.

"Good, I can fuck *you* on the counter this time—wait, did you sanitize before cooking?" they asked.

Milo cackled, peeling himself from around them and walking backwards to the bedroom.

"Milo!"

That evening, Xander came out of the closet in a verdant green velvet button-up shirt, black slacks, and a pair of boots.

"What do you thin—?"

The question fell off Xanders lips about the same time their brain went offline at the sight of Milo.

He was lounged on the bed, leaning back on his palms, legs spread delectably. His curls, however, were half pulled back, a small, loose bun settled atop his head.

Even a few feet apart, Xander could watch his gaze darken as he took in their outfit. He pushed off his palms, leaning forward and propping his forearms on his knees. His button up shirt was rolled up to his elbows, and Xander didn't think they'd ever been so instantly turned on in their entire life.

Milo's grin was downright predatory as he took in the artful gap in their shirt. "I love when you style them like— you good?" he asked, grin slipping into a confused little frown.

It was then that Xander realized their mouth had been open for a while. "I've just… never seen your hair like that," Xander said, voice carefully even.

Milo stood, shuffled his feet and lifted a hand to frame the bun. "Uh, yeah, I guess not." He tucked a finger into the elastic. "I can take it d—"

"No!" Xander answered, a little too quickly. Their cheeks flushed. "Don't do that."

Milo's lips quirked back up as he finally caught on. "Oh, I get it," he purred. "You think I'm hot."

Yes. And Xander kind of wanted to suck his dick about it.

Instead, they scoffed. "What? No. You look fine. Normal, even. And I have totally normal feelings about your… bun." Milo stalked closer with every sputtered word, until he stole the words right off their lips with a kiss.

They lifted their hands to his lapels, gripping them each in their hands as they tilted their head slightly up to meet his kiss with matching vigor.

"It's completely unfair how attractive you are," Xander whispered as they pulled back, gazes clashing with heat. "How are we ever gonna leave the house when all I want to do is..."

"Is...?" Milo prompted, letting his gaze span from their head to their toes. "Go on, finish your sentence."

Xander shook their head, biting their lip to keep the admission contained. "No," they said, stepping back with resolve. "We should leave. It's a date, remember?"

"Alright, whatever you say," Milo agreed, stepping back and fixing his shirt. He shuffled a hand through his curls and Xander swallowed sharply.

"Ready when you are," he said with a teasing grin, and then walked out of the room.

Milo glanced over his shoulder with a knowing smirk and a wink.

Yeah, they were late to the bar.

Milo's bun survived, barely.

Okay fine, maybe he had to restyle it before they left the house, and maybe they were almost *extra* late because apparently Xander was weak for half-bun Milo. Something about watching him carefully collect the curls and wrap the band around them before pulling out the pieces that fell around his face.

A menace is what he was.

Maybe Milo even had to change pants.

One could hardly blame that on Xander. It was *his* cock that leaked so generously. Right through his boxers. And Xander suddenly wondered if even Milo's wardrobe could sustain their libidos.

They looked forward to finding out.

Milo pulled them to a stop before Xander could reach out and open the door of the bar. "So… I have a question first," Milo said, brushing his thumb over the back of their hand.

"What's up?" Xander asked, stomach flipping with sudden nerves.

"When I introduce you, what should I use? Partner?"

Oh.

Xander wondered when they would get used to Milo's absolute acceptance. The more time they spent with him, the more Xander realized they'd never truly known what it was to be accepted. Xander once thought the hunters were the best it got, but Milo proved them wrong with every passing minute.

"Partner is perfect," they agreed casually, as if their whole chest wasn't threatening to crack open from the size of their utter affection.

Milo squeezed their hand, offered a smile that revealed his dimples, and nodded toward the bar. "Ready?"

Xander nodded, because their voice would crack otherwise, and they sucked in a deep breath as Milo opened the door.

Hand in hand, Milo led them inside the bar. It was significantly less crowded than the first time Xander had been there.

"Milo!" Patty cried, and rounded the bar as they walked deeper in. The door slammed shut behind them and Xander followed.

Nerves were bouncing around their chest and they

sucked in a deep breath as Patty engulfed Milo in a bone crushing hug.

Oh god.

Xander was meeting the parents. That's what this was. Patty and John were familial figures to Milo, and he was *introducing* them.

Her gaze locked on Xander, and they felt like a deer caught in headlights. "I remember you," she said, eyes squinting in suspicion.

Xander's heart leapt in their throat.

When she pulled back, her gaze darted from Milo to Xander and back again, the obvious question in her gaze.

Clearing his throat, Milo said, "Patty, this is my partner, Xander. They're new in town."

Xander's nerves dissolved in the sudden brightness that erupted inside them. Bubbly, obnoxious giddiness at the title.

They could float away if they tried.

Thankfully, they had Milo to hang onto, and they squeezed their fingers around his to keep their feet on the floor.

Patty's eyes were probably as wide as Xander's own as she gasped and waved someone over from behind the bar.

"John! John, Milo's finally found a partner! Come meet them!"

"Finally?" Milo questioned, running a hand over the back of his neck. "Come on now…"

Was he blushing? Xander wanted to pinch his cheeks.

"Well, isn't that lovely news," John said, salt and pepper flecked jowls widening in a grin. He held out his hand, and Xander shook. "It's nice to meet you! Come have a drink."

Patty got the glasses and made eyes at them while John poured them both a house ale, and Xander took a sip to swallow down the lump in their throat. If their eyes glistened under the bar lights, no one said a word.

But Milo did squeeze their hand beneath the bar.

"So how did you meet?" Patty asked with a knowing little smile.

Xander glanced over at Milo, found his gaze already locked on them, and matching smiles curled their lips in tandem before they both laughed.

"You won't believe it," Milo said, voice heavy with utter fondness.

Xander's chest ached from the force of affection that fluttered through them.

What a stupid, lovable dragon.

"It started here, actually," Milo began with a wink.

And it's not going to end here, either, Xander thought with conviction.

If Milo thought he was going to fly off and find those dragons by himself, he had another thing coming.

Xander just had to ask him. Nicely.

Maybe warm up to it.

Sure. They could do that.

18. ANYTHING YOU WANT

"I can't take it anymore," Xander blurted suddenly.

Milo stiffened beneath them, heart thumping against his chest at the frustration in their voice.

They were lying together after the bar, letting the ales Patty and John plied them with wear off. Having a good cuddle, or so Milo thought.

"What's wrong?"

Xander huffed. "You haven't asked me to go with you. And I know it goes without saying that I want to help," Xander said. "Finding the dragons."

Milo listened to their heart pick up its pace from where his head rested against their chest. They traced circles into his uninjured shoulder.

"It's only fair, since I'm part of the reason they're all spread out."

Milo… didn't know he could love someone this much, and his panic subsided. "I assumed it was a given, so I'm glad we're on the same page. Did you think I was gonna fly off and leave you here?"

Just the thought made Milo's chest hurt, and it had nothing to do with a stupid magic spell.

"I mean, I don't know. I'd hoped not," Xander admitted.

Pure, indulgent adoration filled him, and he squeezed them tighter.

"I want you to come with me. But I don't even know where to start, to be honest."

Xander's fingers drifted to a stop, and suddenly they were pushing at him. "I do! Shit, Milo move, god," they hissed. Xander practically spilled onto the floor, bare feet squeaking against the hardwood as they ran to the bathroom, robe billowing out behind them.

They returned with their cell phone, fingers tapping on the screen before they held it out to him proudly. "Look."

Brows furrowed, Milo tried to make sense of the data on the screen. A 3-D image of the globe spun on a grid background, little green dots blinking from various locations around the world. "Is that…"

"Last known locations of some of the dragons the HOA was planning to hit." They took the phone back and tapped at the screen some more. "I'm sure I won't have access forever, so I can export the data before… What's your email?"

Clearing his throat, Milo's cheeks were already coloring as he uttered it.

Xander paused, gaze lifting from the device to him, eyes alight with mirth. "Really? Milothedragon at gmail dot com? You're serious?"

"Don't make fun of me," he warned.

They lifted one of their hands in a show of innocence. "I would never," they lied, lips twitching. "Sending the data now, Mr. Obvious."

"Okay, listen—"

"You can't even use the excuse that you were like thirteen, because you were already centuries old when the internet was invented," they laughed.

Milo's lips twitched. "I get it—"

"Oh my god, what do cashiers say when you sign up for

discounts?" They glanced around the lavishly decorated room before shaking their head. "Nevermind, that's silly, you don't need disc—oh!"

Milo yanked them down onto the bed with him, kissing the chuckles right off their lips.

"I'll have you know," he interrupted with another kiss. "I love a good discount."

"I'm just saying, my email isn't xanderthetreasurehunter at whatever dot com," they teased.

"Well, that's just 'cause you're no fun," Milo retorted.

Milo's phone dinged from somewhere in the room, and Xander grinned. "There. Sent. We can use the data to track down some of the dragons, and hopefully beat the hunters to them." They suddenly winced. "I think you should handle the liasoning, since I'm, y'know, a retired hunter and all."

Twining a hand through their hair, Milo hummed. "I think I can vouch for you. And don't worry. I'll still make sure we get our fancy tea and wear the silk robes," Milo muttered. "Even if we are flying all over the place to find the damned dragons."

"You gonna get all sleepy-cute after each flight?"

"Depends. You gonna be there to help carry my ass to the nearest bed?"

Xander hummed, pretending to think about it. "Ehh. Depends on what's in it for me."

Milo wrapped an arm around their waist and pulled them in close. "If I recall, you took quite a liking to my dragon dic—"

Xander slapped a hand over his mouth. "That's not necessary, is it? Bragging is so beneath you."

"I know who I'd rather have beneath me," Milo mouthed, nipping at their palm until they released him. Their hand trailed down his jaw, over his neck to thread through the curls at the back of his head.

They gripped tight, tugged his head back just the slightest bit as they leaned in. "Usually, I'd ask what you've done to earn such a thing," they breathed against his lips.

If Milo wasn't lying down, he would've swayed toward them, but couldn't because of the hand in his hair, and he melted all over again. Xander's expression lit up with mischief, and a spear of heat stabbed Milo's gut.

"Anything," he vowed. "I'll do anything you want."

He couldn't even spare a bit of embarrassment for how true the statement was, and spent the rest of the night proving it.

THE REAL TREASURE

WAS THIS EPILOGUE

"I have a confession to make," Milo said one evening, months later. They were spending a rare weekend at home before they readied for the flight to Europe.

They'd located fifteen dragons over the past few months, and thankfully word was finally beginning to spread. They could come out of hiding, Lucifer wasn't going to kill them for leaving, and the hunters had finally fucked off for good.

Eventually Milo would be able to open his bakery again, and he couldn't wait to teach Xander how to bake every single sugary confection he could think of. Breads, cakes, all of it.

"What's up?" Xander asked, trailing their fingertips over his healed shoulder. The missing scale had grown back, finally, and it was now Xander's favorite place to touch.

Milo lifted his head from his comfortable place on their chest and propped up on his fist, elbow digging into the mattress beside Xander's shoulder. They let their hand drop to the bed, and stared up at him.

"You wanna know where my hoard is?" Milo offered.

Xander blinked up at him before their lips twitched into a smile. "Finally! That's the whole reason I'm here, isn't it?"

Milo rolled his eyes at their sarcasm and the pressure on his chest eased. They had that effect on him.

With a huff, he waved his hand around the room. "Well, you're looking at it."

"I'm sorry, *what?*" Xander blurted, blinking up at him. Their gaze followed his around the room.

Milo couldn't help but laugh at their disbelief, and nodded. "Yep. All the little trinkets and my nice clothes and even that weird looking little mask thing—" He nodded to his left at a tribal mask hanging in the hallway. "It's all shit I've collected through the years. That's my treasure."

"Wait, wait. So you're telling me… you don't have a treasure chest full of gold and jewels from hundreds of years ago like *every other fucking dragon?*" Xander was very still beneath him.

Milo waved his hand. "Please, I had all that converted to zeros decades ago."

Xander sucked in a deep breath. "You didn't even have a hoard to split?"

Their tone was low and dangerous and Milo wondered if he should start running… now?

"Uhm…" Milo pulled his bottom lip between his teeth, fighting a smile. "Not one that wouldn't have drawn the attention of my accountant?"

Xander pushed at his shoulder, following him as he rolled over until they were settled atop him, both hands pressing into his chest.

"Well, you've spoiled all my plans now," Xander said with a sigh.

"What plans are those?" Milo asked.

"I mean this long con, it's all for nothing," Xander whined, throwing their hands up in the air before crossing them over their chest.

Milo choked on his laugh. "Oh, right. Sorry. Didn't mean to ruin it all."

As if he hadn't spent the last few months spoiling Xander with every cent in his wallet just to see their eyes light up. As if Xander hadn't loved every fucking second of it. Traveling so much meant showing Xander every one of his favorite places, finding new shops and dressing them in every vibrant color he could find. Milo had kissed them on the highest of mountains and wrapped his arms around their waist in cities surrounded by the tallest points.

Even now, one of their new robes framed their shoulders, resting across their back and pooling on top of Milo's thighs. It was black, making all their bare, pale skin glow in contrast.

His hoard would last him several lifetimes. He didn't mind spending a few of them on the love of his life.

"How are you gonna make it up to me then?" Xander asked. They adjusted their weight across Milo's hips instinctively, and Milo… Well, Milo was just a dragon.

Couldn't exactly blame him for framing their waist and dragging them harder against his happy scales.

Their act faltered as they sucked in a breath. "Careful, Milo," they warned, dark and dangerous.

Milo suddenly wanted to be anything but careful.

"Don't you need to rest before the flight Monday? It's a long one, isn't it?"

"We have the rest of our lives to rest, don't we?" he asked, trying to coax Xander down to him. "We're only home so many weekends. Don't we wanna… make the most of it?"

Milo was already hard beneath them, and they hitched their hips back, grinding their ass against him experimentally.

"You drive a hard bargain," Xander said, planting their palms on either side of his head, finally dropping their lips against his.

"I bet you drive a harder one," Milo retorted into the kiss, hands threading through their hair.

They paused suddenly, pulling back to stare down at him. "D'you mean…"

Milo nodded. "Yes. Yes, I do mean."

"Fuck. Shit. Okay," Xander said, nodding and interrupting the kiss.

They'd tried a few different toys over the recent months. Some they'd unwrapped together and giggled at until tears streamed down their cheeks.

Apparently *dragon dildos* did not always return the same results.

"In the mood for a specific one?" Xander asked as they pulled a leg over his hip to reach under the bed.

Milo stared at the long, stretched line of their body appreciatively. "You pick," he murmured, distracted.

Xander glanced over their shoulder, catching Milo's shameless stare. The wink they sent was nothing less than devastating.

"Like what you see?" they asked, before sliding off the bed. Each movement was calculated, smooth and precise.

When Milo shuffled across the mattress to assist in strapping them up, Xander held out a hand.

"No, stay there. You can watch." It came out like an order, and a swell of heat crashed over him, cock pulsing to life in anticipation.

Milo drew in a silent breath and settled back against the pillows. "Okay," he choked out.

The fucking robe obscured most of his view, only offering the scarcest glimpses. Miles of pale skin beneath the shiny silk of the robe, black leather straps that reminded Milo of all the harnesses Xander liked to wear across their chest.

Personally, these straps were Milo's favorite. The way

they cupped Xander's ass was downright sinful, *and* these straps always came with… attachments.

The robe ruffled to stillness as Xander finished, and they glanced over their shoulder once more.

Before Milo could see what they'd be working with that evening, Xander tightened the robe around their waist and crawled onto the bed, situating between Milo's thighs with a sly grin.

"Keeping secrets tonight, are we?" he said, trying not to let eagerness seep into his voice. Cool, calm, collected. Not at all like he couldn't wait for Xander to fuck every thought out of his head.

"Just for a bit. I picked one of your favorites."

Milo arched a brow. "And which one is that?"

Xander shrugged, lips curled into a cocky little smirk that they pressed to his hipbone.

"Guess you'll find out."

Milo rolled his eyes, and paused as a thought occurred to him. "Do you think I could tell just from the feel of it?"

Xander's gaze flicked up to his, hazel eyes heating as they flattened their palms on his thighs and dragged their nails through the dark hairs. He sucked in a breath as chills spread in their wake.

"I bet I could," Milo challenged, a little more breathlessly.

"Is that a game you wanna play? I bet you'll lose," Xander retorted.

Oh, Xander knew how to play him just right. Milo narrowed his gaze, and tapped their hip with his foot. "Game on."

With a grin, Xander leaned down and nipped at the sensitive skin of his thigh, and Milo's cock twitched. Xander usually was the first to wrap their hand around him, but instead, they were taking their time.

They kissed and nipped and teased his chest and hips and

thighs and Milo was a shivery, desperate mess by the time Xander drifted close to his cock.

He froze in anticipation as their breath warmed the head of him, their gaze flashing up to him, dangerously smug.

"Touch me," Milo said, voice rough with arousal.

At their single, arched brow, he choked out, "Please."

A shout punched from his throat as they wrapped their fingers around him. Their grip was tight and perfect as they stroked him, and his mouth fell open on a groan as their fist closed over the head of him. Milo watched the precum well in abundance, pooling and spilling over the circle they made with their thumb and forefinger.

And too soon their touch left him, but it drifted down and he forgot to be disappointed as pure eagerness delighted him. Xander trailed their wet fingers where he wanted them most, and he brought one knee up, creating more space for them to—

Xander's touch was never less than ruinous, and Milo was desperate to be ruined by them.

Over and over and forever.

His stomach clenched at the first brush of their finger against him.

If he thought Xander was suddenly going to speed up, give him what he wanted when he wanted it, he was delight-fully mistaken.

Xander teased him mercilessly, caressing the pad of their fingers over his hole, spreading his own wetness, alternating sure strokes of his cock when they needed more slick.

Milo groaned on the third pass of this torture. "Xander, come *on*," he begged, horny frustration lacing his tone.

Xander paused. "What was that?" they asked too sweetly.

Milo gulped. "If you don't put your fingers in me I'm going to *die*," he complained.

If Xander's lips twitched, they did a very good job of

hiding it by dropping their mouth around his cock, and any complaint Milo had was expelled on a moan.

He fisted the sheets as Xander finally, *finally* entered him with just one finger, and it wasn't enough—was it ever?—and slid in to the first knuckle.

"More," Milo whined, all thought of composure flying out the window along with his sanity as Xander forged deeper.

Xander sucked around his cock, cheeks hollowing at the same time they withdrew, and Milo's entire body jolted.

"Fuck," he hissed, eyes fluttering shut at the way Xander played him like an instrument. "You're too—ah, ah —powerful," he groaned.

Xander pulled off his cock, and chuckled against his hip before they dipped their head lower.

"What're you—oh fuck." The words choked out of him as Xander pursed their lips and let the arousal they'd collected spill out over their fingers. "God, you're so fucking hot." They were gonna be the death of him.

And what a fucking death it would be, too.

Milo rocked his hips into their touch as they returned with two fingers, sliding in easily, but taking their time because they were *evil.* They parted their fingers, stretching him open and sliding in deeper, crooking their fingers until—

"*Fuck*—me," Milo ground out, body surging. His leg fell to the side and he didn't fucking care.

"I'm trying to," Xander purred, and Milo melted against the bed as much as he could, body tense because Xander kept… kept brushing their fingers inside him.

Pleasure echoed through him in waves, turning his mind to static.

"Come on, Xander, I'm ready—you know it," he panted, locking onto their gaze.

Their cheeks and chest were flushed, and Xander pushed his other leg up, locking their palm behind his knee.

"Oh," Milo croaked out. Xander *was* going to ruin him.

"Close your eyes," Xander said.

Right, the game.

He let his head fall to the bed, eyes fluttering shut. They *almost* flew open as Xander wrapped their hand back around his length, but he was *good* dammit, and did little more than pant into the air and anticipate Xander's next touch.

"Relax," they whispered as their hand disappeared, voice all velvet purr and—

The head of them brushed against Milo and his breath escaped on a shudder, following their direction.

"D'you know why I picked this one?" they asked softly.

Milo shook his head, grip tightening around the sheets as they slowly forged forward. His lips parted as Xander's hips rocked, so gently, almost too gently, as they slid in.

He tried to focus on the shape, the feel, because they were both competitive and Milo wanted to *win.* But *fuuuck,* it felt so good.

"Tapered?" Milo asked as they rocked in another inch or so. It spread him wider as they went.

He could *hear* the smugness in their grin. "Yeah." But their voice was rough and fuck, the knowing. Knowing that Xander was watching Milo lose his shit and getting off on it was downright heady.

Xander wrapped a hand around his cock again, stroking firm and slow, to the same rhythm they rocked their hips, teasing Milo more than fucking him, easing him onto the silicone one short thrust at a time.

He wet his dry lips, concentrating, or trying to. Instead, he kept losing himself in the pleasure, the stretch and the... the ridges that slid inside him only to pull at his entrance on the way back out.

"Textured?" he questioned, the word barely a breath.

Xander sounded slightly less smug. "Yes."

Milo almost chuckled, almost—if they hadn't thrust in a little harder, given him more of what he wanted.

"Are you glaring at me?" Milo asked, his voice breaking as humor and pleasure warred.

"No, Baby, why would you think that?"

Not the pet names, oh god. Milo melted into the mattress at Xander's chuckle, and he lifted a hand from the sheets to grab—there!

Silk slid through his fingers as he gripped at Xander's robe. He *loved* when they fucked him while wearing it. Any of them. All of them. Hell, at the same time, who was he to say?

He shivered, wished he could open his eyes and— "I wanna see you," he breathed.

"Not yet," they responded. "No cheating."

But their pace increased, and Milo groaned and arched beneath them as they worked inch after inch into him. By the time their hips clapped against his own, Milo had to warn their hand away from his cock because he was going to come and it was far too soon.

After all, he hadn't figured out what toy it was.

"You can look now."

They withdrew their hips as Milo obeyed, and fucked a shout right from his lips as he blinked his eyes open.

Their hair was a dark, wild frame around their flushed face, eyes melting him to the spot with the intensity of their gaze.

He studied them, the robe falling off one shoulder, the dark fabric outlining them against the soft light from the hall.

"Eyes on me," they breathed when his gaze dared to dip lower, and he shifted his focus.

Milo released his grip on the robe with a flutter as he

threaded a hand through their mussed hair and pulled them down.

It changed the angle, and Milo moaned just as their lips met. Xander took advantage and licked into his mouth, and Milo met them with desperate fervor.

"Ready?" they asked.

"You gonna destroy me now?" he asked, and didn't do a very good job of keeping the neediness out of his voice.

"Yeah. Definitely," Xander replied, hips already moving.

The texture was... Milo didn't even know how to describe it.

Ribbed for his pleasure, he thought a little deliriously.

The way it slid in so easily but tugged at his entrance on each withdrawal was intoxicating, and the sounds it pulled from him could have been embarrassing if not for the way it only encouraged Xander.

"Is it the b-blue one?" Milo asked, breath weak as it spilled from his chest on a harsh thrust.

Xander shook their head, slamming their hips into him in a rhythm that made him see stars.

"Red one," he guessed.

"No. Wanna know why I picked this one?" they asked, voice as breathless as Milo's.

Milo's eyes went wide, still locked on Xander. "Why?"

"It reminded me... of the blue one. You always sound..." Their expression crumpled as they rocked into him, and Milo wondered what they'd chosen for themself to grind against. The break in their words was punctuated with another thrust. "When we use the blue one, you get desperate." Their eyes flashed open. "I want you desperate."

"What are you using?" Milo asked, because he had to know. It was suddenly the only thing he could think about.

Xander's lips twitched, and Milo grabbed at their thigh with one hand, fingers squeezing on every thrust. Their lids drifted shut briefly, but Milo didn't call them on it because he was too enamored by the ecstasy in their expression. "The pink grinder?" he asked, because it was their favorite.

They met his gaze again as they nodded, lips parted, and Milo pulled them back down for a kiss. Their hand slid from behind his knee to plant on the bed, and Milo groaned at the shift in angle. They felt bigger inside him, and on the next thrust he was helpless but to whine.

"There," Xander breathed, and they fucked him harder.

Xander nipped at his jaw as they panted together, as the edge neared, as they rocked each other into oblivion.

Whatever new shape this was, Milo loved it, and he didn't even care about the game anymore. He just wanted *more* of Xander.

"Look at me," Xander said suddenly.

Milo blinked his eyes open—fuck, he didn't even notice they'd closed—to Xander's wide blown eyes. "Is this one your new favorite?" they asked.

Milo could only nod as they increased the pace, and all previous thought blanked his mind as they drove into him again and again.

Pleasure fizzled along his senses, drove up his spine and pulsed with every thrust of their hips.

"More," Milo demanded, and Xander worked a hand between them.

Milo shouted as their knuckles brushed his stomach on the first stroke.

"God, you feel so good," Xander whispered. "You're so wet for it," they continued. "I love when you get like this."

This must refer to the whining mess they turned Milo into, pleas spilling out with every plunge.

"Come on," Xander coaxed. "Eyes on me, come for me Baby."

Oh *fuck*.

Milo didn't even have to question what sent him over the edge.

If it was the mysterious ridges in the silicone, or the deliciously harsh thrusts or just watching Xander grind themself to the edge on Milo's own pleasure.

He shouted as he came, spilling hot and perfect over Xander's fist. At first they fucked him through it, but then the pleasure took them too. Milo felt it with their whole body, the way they tensed against him, freezing for a split second before a moan tumbled out, hips smacking against him with a slow, soft renewed fervor.

Their expression furrowed, but their gaze remained intense on him as they watched each other go over the edge. The rhythm slowed, stalled out, and Milo pulled them to him, tasting the pleasure straight from the source.

Their stomachs slicked against one another from his mess, but neither of them could be bothered.

Words were scarce, and Milo's brain was still offline by the time Xander chuckled.

"Did you figure it out?"

Milo's lips twitched, and he let his legs fall to bed, limp. "Fuck. No. I forgot," he admitted.

Xander kissed him again, and Milo hummed, positively captivated by his treasure hunter.

"You probably could've guessed it. If it wasn't new."

Milo sputtered. "Wh-what is it?"

"It's…" Xander sat up, and slowly inched their hips apart. He swallowed sharply at the shimmer on their stomach, covered in him.

Then his attention dropped lower.

"Where… did you find *that*?" Milo asked, staring down at a dildo that was suspiciously shaped like his own dick.

"I found a new company that makes dildos similar to *real* supernatural creatures. This was on there."

"You fucked me with my own dick," Milo deadpanned. It was tapered and textured just like his own. The only difference was the color, which was bright, sparkly purple.

"And you *liked it*," Xander retorted proudly.

"Maybe I just liked the person attached to it," he suggested.

Xander hummed doubtfully, and Milo pulled them back down to him, tongues twining until they forgot what they were talking about.

It wasn't long before they were a little too messy even for their own tastes, and Xander urged them into the shower.

By the time they returned and remade the bed, they were warm and sleepy and collapsed together on the pillows.

Xander rested their head on his chest and Milo tucked his hand into their hair, breaths synching on a soft rise and fall.

"I'm glad you told me about your hoard," Xander said. "Though I thought you were gonna have something cool like a secret room only accessible if you pull the right book. Or something."

That was oddly specific. His lips twitched.

"Thought about this a lot, have you?"

"What? No. Of course not," they said as they propped their chin on his chest. "Besides. Maybe the real treasure was the... y'know," they said, motioning between them as their cheeks flushed bright, eyes sparkling. "Us," Xander muttered. They winced and rolled off his chest, burying their face in the pillows.

Milo melted, and shook their shoulder. "Aww, Sunshine. You *love* me," he teased. Xander hated, but secretly loved, when he called them that.

"Do not," they lied, speaking into the pillow. "I'm suffocating myself. I can't believe I—"

Milo yanked the pillow from beneath their head as they finished saying, "said that."

"I can. You *love* me," he said, dragging out the syllables.

Xander's gaze narrowed, though their smile was slipping through. They snatched the pillow back, and brandished it like a weapon. "There won't be anything left to love once I'm through with you."

"Oh, don't threaten me with a good time," he retorted, heart swelling like the giant sap he'd become.

They whopped him once with the pillow before a chuckle broke free, and then chased him down to the mattress with a kiss.

"Dildos are kind of a cool treasure too, y'know," Milo said.

Xander sighed as if they'd known he was going to say it, and were just biding their time. "We have enough, don't we?"

"Could always get more," he suggested.

Xander hummed, cracking one eye open and arching a brow at him. "There was quite a collection available on that website."

Milo cleared his throat. "Just out of curiosity, what other types of supernaturals were available?"

"Oh, all kinds," Xander assured him, and closed their eyes again.

He tapped his fingers against their shoulder blade. "But specifically... what kinds?" he tried again.

Xander shook against him for a moment before more chuckles burst out, and Milo's smile curled in a grin.

"God, I love you so much, y'know?" Xander admitted, suddenly soft. "You're ridiculous."

"You're more ridiculous."

"Most ridiculous," they retorted.

"Oh, I don't know about that," Milo argued. "I mean, the *real* treasure was the love we found along the way, right?"

Milo couldn't tell if Xander wanted to choke him or kiss him more.

Little did they know he was down for both.

AFTERWORD

Meowdy!!
So… what did you think? (eye emojis)
This story is very close to my heart, especially with current
happenings.
Stories are supposed to be our escape, and I hope I offered
you a bit of that with this book.
Much love,
Lana

ACKNOWLEDGMENTS

I cannot thank my sensitivity readers enough for being so open to questions and sharing pieces of themselves with me as this story was molded into its current form.

Thank you Meg for squeeing over these characters and being excited about this story every step of the way.

Thank you Sonny for sending me cat pics of Kabachok and Lyosha and creating the loveliest art for my brain babies.

And thank you to all my Patrons for your support!

ALSO BY

Visit my website to learn more about my books and how to get your paws on signed paperbacks.

www.lanakoleauthor.com

Cautionary Tails Series

How Not to Date a Demon

How Not to Date a Dragon

How Not to Date a Griffin

How Not to Date an Angel

Short & Sweets

Seasonal Spice & Everything Nice 1

Seasonal Spice & Everything Nice 2

Seasonal Spice & Everything Nice 3

Monster Vacation Series

The Abdominal Snowman

Tentacle Difficulties

In the Sweetverse w/ Kathryn Moon

Baby + the Late Night Howlers

Lola & the Millionaires Part One

Lola & the Millionaires Part Two

Lyric & the Heartbeats

Fighting Instincts

Bad Alpha

All Packed Up

Faith + the Dead End Devils

Knot That Serious

Ashley & the A-Listers

Crystal Clear Series

Illusion of Escape

Illusion of Death

Illusion of Darkness

The Unlocked Series

Chaos Unlocked

Betrayal Exposed

Misery Undone

Truth Revealed

Hope Lost

Death Defied

Standalones

Feline Good

LANA KOLE WRITING AS LOGAN GREY

Heartbelt Records Series

The Deeper You Go

The Longer You'll Stay

Love in Progress

ABOUT *the* AUTHOR

With a southern twang that's all charm, Lana Kole hails from Tennessee with their four feline roommates. Lana's most likely busy writing stories, but not without a cat purring in their lap. Their work brings life to characters who don't fit the mold, romance as sweet as it is sexy, and worlds better than this one.
Author of paranormal, sweet omegaverse, monster romance, and queer love stories with a happily ever after.